A Mussoor

Ruskin Bond has been writing for over sixty years, and now has over 120 titles in print—novels, collections of short stories, poetry, essays, anthologies and books for children. His first novel, *The Room on the Roof*, received the prestigious John Llewellyn Rhys Prize in 1957. He has also received the Padma Shri (1999), the Padma Bhushan (2014) and two awards from Sahitya Akademi—one for his short stories and another for his writings for children. In 2012, the Delhi government gave him its Lifetime Achievement Award.

Born in 1934, Ruskin Bond grew up in Jamnagar, Shimla, New Delhi and Dehradun. Apart from three years in the UK, he has spent all his life in India, and now lives in Mussoorie with his adopted family.

A Mussoorie Mystery

Edited and Compiled by
RUSKIN BOND

RUPA

Published by
Rupa Publications India Pvt. Ltd 2017
7/16, Ansari Road, Daryaganj
New Delhi 110002

Sales centres:
Allahabad Bengaluru Chennai
Hyderabad Jaipur Kathmandu
Kolkata Mumbai

ISBN: 978-81-291-3582-7

First impression 2017

10 9 8 7 6 5 4 3 2 1

Printed at Thomson Press India Ltd., Faridabad

Contents

Introduction

'Mr Bond, do suggest a book that I can read.' Or 'Mr Bond, it's been so long since I have read a novel, but I do wish to read regularly again. What should I do?'

These are questions that are asked of me often, as I sit at the bookstore on the mall in Mussoorie and meet my readers who queue up to get their copies of books signed. I am tempted to point them to the stacks of copies of my books lying on the bookshelves of the store, but then seeing the hopeful look in their eyes, I pause to think a bit. I then end up suggesting a good collection of short stories to many of them. Whether one is a voracious reader or an occasional one, there are very few who don't get a great feeling of satisfaction from reading a good short story.

What makes a good short story, could be the next question. Sharply described characters who come to life with just a few strokes of the pen, a tight plot that doesn't meander and deviate and even when it seems to do so, there's a reason for it, and importantly, a plausible and good ending. Not all endings can be as twisted as the ones thought of by H.H. Munroe, or Saki as he was better known, but there should be something right there at the very end of the story that makes the reader sit up and think for a while.

In this collection, there are stories that come from various genres. My one thought while picking them was that they should be excellent short stories. So there are stories here by Ambrose Bierce and Saki, both masters of their craft. Bierce was American and excelled in stories that dealt with dark themes and horror. Unlike Poe, he also infused them with satire and gave them humorous twists. His book *The Devil's Dictionary* is one such example of masterful dark comedy.

O. Henry was another master of the short form. Included here is his evergreen classic 'The Gift of the Magi'. One never tires of reading this story of the couple out to get the perfect gift for each other and the surprising twist in the end. Jerome K. Jerome was a humour writer whose 'Three Men in a Boat' is read widely even today. Here, you will find his story about a robotic dancing partner that is as bizarre as it is satirical. And then there is Mark Twain, whose stories, essays, novels proclaimed a sharp wit and sharp tongue and who remains a quotable writer even today.

Fantastic, scary, surprising or humorous, the stories in this collection are bound to bring forth all kinds of emotions. I do hope the reader enjoys each one of them and if it inspires them to read more then I hope I would have answered that oft-repeated question finally.

Ruskin Bond

The Gift of the Magi

O. Henry

One dollar and eighty-seven cents. That was all. And sixty cents of it was in pennies. Pennies saved one or two at a time by bulldozing the grocer and the vegetable man and the butcher until one's cheek burned with the silent imputation of parsimony that such close dealing implied. Three times Della counted it. One dollar and eighty-seven cents. And the next day would be Christmas.

There was clearly nothing left to do but flop down on the shabby little couch and howl. So Della did it. Which instigates the moral reflection that life is made up of sobs, sniffles and smiles, with sniffles predominating.

While the mistress of the home is gradually subsiding from the first stage to the second, take a look at the home. A furnished flat at $8 per week. It did not exactly beggar description, but it certainly had that word on the look-out for the mendicancy squad.

In the vestibule below was a letter-box into which no letter would go, and an electric button from which no mortal finger could coax a ring. Also appertaining thereunto was a card bearing the name 'Mr James Dillingham Young'.

The 'Dillingham' had been flung to the breeze during a former period of prosperity when its possessor was being paid $30 per week. Now, when the income was shrunk to $20, the letters of 'Dillingham' looked blurred, as though they were thinking seriously of contracting to a modest and unassuming D. But whenever Mr James Dillingham Young came home and reached his flat above he was called 'Jim' and greatly hugged by Mrs James Dillingham Young, already introduced to you as Della. Which is all very good.

Della finished her cry and attended to her cheeks with the powder rag. She stood by the window and looked out dully at a grey cat walking a grey fence in a grey backyard. Tomorrow would be Christmas Day, and she had only $1.87 with which to buy Jim a present. She had been saving every penny she could for months, with this result. Twenty dollars a week doesn't go far. Expenses had been greater than she had calculated. They always are. Only $1.87 to buy a present for Jim. Her Jim. Many a happy hour she had spent planning for something nice for him. Something fine and rare and sterling—something just a little bit near to being worthy of the honour of being owned by Jim.

There was a pier-glass between the windows of the room. Perhaps you have seen a pier-glass in an $8 flat. A very thin and very agile person may, by observing his reflection in a rapid sequence of longitudinal strips, obtain a fairly accurate conception of his looks. Della, being slender, had mastered the art.

Suddenly she whirled from the window and stood before the glass. Her eyes were shining brilliantly, but her face had lost its colour within twenty seconds. Rapidly she pulled down her hair and let it fall to its full length.

Now, there were two possessions of the James Dillingham Youngs in which they both took a mighty pride. One was Jim's gold watch that had been his father's and his grandfather's. The other was Della's hair. Had the Queen of Sheba lived in the flat across the airshaft, Della would have let her hair hang out the window some day to dry just to depreciate Her Majesty's jewels and gifts. Had King Solomon been the janitor, with all his treasures piled up in the basement, Jim would have pulled out his watch every time he passed, just to see him pluck at his beard from envy.

So now Della's beautiful hair fell about her, rippling and shining like a cascade of brown waters. It reached below her knee and made itself almost a garment for her. And then she did it up again nervously and quickly. Once she faltered for a minute and stood still while a tear or two splashed on the worn red carpet.

On went her old brown jacket; on went her old brown hat. With a whirl of skirts and with the brilliant sparkle still in her eyes, she fluttered out of the door and down the stairs to the street.

Where she stopped the sign read: 'Mme. Sofronie. Hair Goods of All Kinds'. One flight up Della ran, and collected herself, panting. Madame, large, too white, chilly, hardly looked the 'Sofronie'.

'Will you buy my hair?' asked Della.

'I buy hair,' said Madame. 'Take yer hat off and let's have a sight at the looks of it.'

Down rippled the brown cascade.

'Twenty dollars,' said Madame, lifting the mass with a practised hand.

'Give it to me quick,' said Della.

Oh, and the next two hours tripped by on rosy wings. Forget the hashed metaphor. She was ransacking the stores for Jim's present.

She found it at last. It surely had been made for Jim and no one else. There was no other like it in any of the stores, and she had turned all of them inside out. It was a platinum fob chain simple and chaste in design, properly proclaiming its value by substance alone and not by meretricious ornamentation—as all good things should do. It was even worthy of The Watch. As soon as she saw it she knew that it must be Jim's. It was like him. Quietness and value—the description applied to both. Twenty-one dollars they took from her for it, and she hurried home with the 87 cents. With that chain on his watch Jim might be properly anxious about the time in any company. Grand as the watch was, he sometimes looked at it on the sly on account of the old leather strap that he used in place of a chain.

When Della reached home her intoxication gave way a little to prudence and reason. She got out her curling irons and lighted the gas and went to work repairing the ravages made by generosity added to love. Which is always a tremendous task, dear friends—a mammoth task.

Within forty minutes her head was covered with tiny, close-lying curls that made her look wonderfully like a truant schoolboy. She looked at her reflection in the mirror long, carefully and critically.

'If Jim doesn't kill me,' she said to herself, 'before he takes a second look at me, he'll say I look like a Coney Island chorus girl. But what could I do—oh! What could I do with a dollar and eighty-seven cents?'

At seven o'clock the coffee was made and the frying-pan was on the back of the stove, hot and ready to cook the chops.

Jim was never late. Della doubled the fob chain in her hand and sat on the corner of the table near the door that he always entered. Then she heard his step on the stairway down on the first flight, and she turned white for just a moment. She had a habit of saying little silent prayers about the simplest everyday things, and now she whispered: 'Please God, make him think I am still pretty.'

The door opened and Jim stepped in and closed it. He looked thin and very serious. Poor fellow, he was only twenty-two and to be burdened with a family! He needed a new overcoat and he was without gloves.

Jim stepped inside the door, as immovable as a setter at the scent of quail. His eyes were fixed upon Della, and there was an expression in them that she could not read, and it terrified her. It was not anger, nor surprise, nor disapproval, nor horror, nor any of the sentiments that she had been prepared for. He simply stared at her fixedly with that peculiar expression on his face.

Della wriggled off the table and went for him.

'Jim, darling,' she cried, 'don't look at me that way. I had my hair cut off and sold it because I couldn't have lived through Christmas without giving you a present. It'll grow out again—you won't mind, will you? I just had to do it. My hair grows awfully fast. Say "Merry Christmas!" Jim, and let's be happy.

You don't know what a nice—what a beautiful, nice gift I've got for you.'

'You've cut off your hair?' asked Jim, laboriously, as if he had not arrived at that patent fact yet even after the hardest mental labour.

'Cut it off and sold it,' said Della. 'Don't you like me just as well, anyhow? I'm me without my hair, ain't I?'

Jim looked about the room curiously.

'You say your hair is gone?' he said with an air almost of idiocy.

'You needn't look for it,' said Della. 'It's sold, I tell you—sold and gone, too. It's Christmas Eve, boy. Be good to me, for it went for you. Maybe the hair of my head were numbered,' she went on with a sudden serious sweetness, 'but nobody could ever count my love for you. Shall I put the chops on, Jim?'

Out of his trance Jim seemed quickly to wake. He enfolded his Della. For ten seconds let us regard with discreet scrutiny some inconsequential object in the other direction. Eight dollars a week or a million a year—what is the difference? A mathematician or a wit would give you the wrong answer. The magi brought valuable gifts, but that was not among them. This dark assertion will be illuminated later on.

Jim drew a package from his overcoat pocket and threw it upon the table.

'Don't make any mistake, Dell,' he said, 'about me. I don't think there's anything in the way of a haircut or a shave or a shampoo that could make me like my girl any less. But if you'll unwrap that package you may see why you had me going awhile at first.'

White fingers and nimble tore at the string and paper. And then an ecstatic scream of joy; and then, alas! a quick feminine change to hysterical tears and wails, necessitating the immediate employment of all the comforting powers of the lord of the flat.

For there lay The Combs—the set of combs, side and back, that Della had worshipped for long in a Broadway window. Beautiful combs, pure tortoise-shell, with jewelled rims—just the shade to wear in the beautiful vanished hair. They were expensive combs, she knew, and her heart had simply craved and yearned over them without the least hope of possession. And now they were hers, but the tresses that should have adorned the coveted adornments were gone.

But she hugged them to her bosom, and at length she was able to look up with dim eyes and a smile and *say:* 'My hair grows so fast, Jim!'

And then Della leaped up like a little singed cat and cried, 'Oh, oh!'

Jim had not yet seen his beautiful present. She held it out to him eagerly upon her open palm. The dull precious metal seemed to flash with a reflection of her bright and ardent spirit.

'Isn't it a dandy, Jim? I hunted all over town to find it. You'll have to look at the time a hundred times a day now. Give me your watch. I want to see how it looks on it.'

Instead of obeying, Jim tumbled down on the couch and put his hands under the back of his head and smiled.

'Dell,' said he, 'let's put our Christmas presents away and keep 'em awhile. They're too nice to use just at present. I sold the watch to get the money to buy your combs. And now suppose you put the chops on.'

The magi, as you know, were wise men—wonderfully wise men—who brought gifts to the Babe in the manger. They invented the art of giving Christmas presents. Being wise, their gifts were no doubt wise ones, possibly bearing the privilege of exchange in case of duplication. And here I have lamely related to you the uneventful chronicle of two foolish children in a flat who most unwisely sacrificed for each other the greatest treasures of their house. But in a last word to the wise of these days, let it be said that of all who give gifts these two were the wisest. Of all who give and receive gifts, such as they are wisest. Everywhere they are wisest. They are the magi.

The Dancing Partner

Jerome K. Jerome

'This story,' commenced MacShaugnassy, 'comes from Furtwangen, a small town in the Black Forest. There lived there a very wonderful old fellow named Nicholaus Geibel. His business was the making of mechanical toys, at which work he had acquired an almost European reputation. He made rabbits that would emerge from the heart of a cabbage, flop their ears, smooth their whiskers, and disappear again; cats that would wash their faces, and mew so naturally that dogs would mistake them for real cats and fly at them; dolls with phonographs concealed within them, that would raise their hats and say, 'Good morning; how do you do?' and some that would even sing a song.

'But, he was something more than a mere mechanic; he was an artist. His work was with him a hobby, almost a passion. His shop was filled with all manner of strange things that never would, or could, be sold—things he had made for the pure love of making them. He had contrived a mechanical donkey that would trot for two hours by means of stored electricity, and trot, too, much faster than the live article, and with less need for exertion on the part of the driver, a bird that would shoot up into the air, fly round and round in a circle, and drop to earth at the exact spot from where it started; a skeleton that, supported by an upright iron bar, would dance a hornpipe, a life-size lady doll that could play the fiddle, and a gentleman with a hollow inside who could smoke a pipe and drink more lager beer than any three average German students put together, which is saying much.

'Indeed, it was the belief of the town that old Geibel could make a man capable of doing everything that a respectable man need want to do. One day he made a man who did too much, and it came about in this way:

'Young Doctor Follen had a baby, and the baby had a birthday. Its first birthday put Doctor Follen's household into somewhat of a flurry, but on the occasion of its second birthday, Mrs Doctor Follen gave a ball in honour of the event. Old Geibel and his daughter Olga were among the guests.

'During the afternoon of the next day some three or four of Olga's bosom friends, who had also been present at the ball, dropped in to have a chat about it. They naturally fell to discussing the men, and to criticizing their dancing. Old Geibel was in the room, but he appeared to be absorbed in his newspaper, and the girls took no notice of him.

'"There seem to be fewer men who can dance at every ball you go to," said one of the girls.

'"Yes, and don't the ones who can give themselves airs," said another; "they make quite a favour of asking you."

'"And how stupidly they talk," added a third. "They always

say exactly the same things: 'How charming you are looking tonight.' 'Do you often go to Vienna? Oh, you should, it's delightful.' 'What a charming dress you have on.' 'What a warm day it has been.' 'Do you like Wagner?' I do wish they'd think of something new."

"'Oh, I never mind how they talk," said a fourth. "If a man dances well he may be a fool for all I care."

"'He generally is," slipped in a thin girl, rather spitefully.

"'I go to a ball to dance," continued the previous speaker, not noticing the interruption. "All I ask is that he shall hold me firmly, take me round steadily, and not get tired before I do."

"'A clockwork figure would be the thing for you," said the girl who had interrupted.

"'Bravo!" cried one of the others, clapping her hands, "what a capital idea!"

"'What's a capital idea?" they asked.

"'Why, a clockwork dancer, or, better still, one that would go by electricity and never run down."

'The girls took up the idea with enthusiasm.

"'Oh, what a lovely partner he would make," said one; "he would never kick you, or tread on your toes."

"'Or tear your dress," said another.

"'Or get out of step."

"'Or get giddy and lean on you."

"'And he would never want to mop his face with his handkerchief. I do hate to see a man do that after every dance."

"'And wouldn't want to spend the whole evening in the supper-room."

"'Why, with a phonograph inside him to grind out all the

stock remarks, you would not be able to tell him from a real man," said the girl who had first suggested the idea.

'"Oh yes, you would," said the thin girl, "he would be so much nicer."

'Old Geibel had laid down his paper, and was listening with both his ears. On one of the girls glancing in his direction, however, he hurriedly hid himself again behind it.

'After the girls were gone, he went into his workshop, where Olga heard him walking up and down, and every now and then chuckling to himself; and that night he talked to her a good deal about dancing and dancing men—asked what dances were most popular—what steps were gone through, with many other questions bearing on the subject.

'Then for a couple of weeks he kept much to his factory, and was very thoughtful and busy, though prone at unexpected moments to break into a quiet low laugh, as if enjoying a joke that nobody else knew of.

'A month later another ball took place in Furtwangen. On this occasion it was given by old Wenzel, the wealthy timber merchant, to celebrate his niece's betrothal, and Geibel and his daughter were again among the invited.

'When the hour arrived to set out, Olga sought her father. Not finding him in the house, she tapped at the door of his workshop. He appeared in his shirt-sleeves, looking hot but radiant.

'"Don't wait for me," he said, "you go on, I'll follow you. I've got something to finish."

'As she turned to obey he called after her, "Tell them I'm going to bring a young man with me—such a nice young man, and an excellent dancer. All the girls will like him." Then he laughed and closed the door.

'Her father generally kept his doings secret from everybody, but she had a pretty shrewd suspicion of what he had been planning, and so, to a certain extent, was able to prepare the guests for what was coming. Anticipation ran high, and the arrival of the famous mechanist was eagerly awaited.

'At length the sound of wheels was heard outside, followed by a great commotion in the passage, and old Wenzel himself, his jolly face red with excitement and suppressed laughter, burst into the room and announced in stentorian tones:

'"Herr Geibel—and a friend."

'Herr Geibel and his "friend" entered, greeted with shouts of laughter and applause, and advanced to the centre of the room.

'"Allow me, ladies and gentlemen," said Herr Geibel, "to introduce you to my friend, Lieutenant Fritz. Fritz, my dear fellow, bow to the ladies and gentlemen."

'Geibel placed his hand encouragingly on Fritz's shoulder, and the Lieutenant bowed low, accompanying the action with a harsh clicking noise in his throat, unpleasantly suggestive of a death-rattle. But that was only a detail.

'"He walks a little stiffly" (old Geibel took his arm and walked him forward a few steps. He certainly did walk stiffly), "But then, walking is not his forte. He is essentially a dancing man. I have only been able to teach him the waltz as yet, but at that he is faultless. Come, which of you ladies may I introduce him to as a partner? He keeps perfect time; he never gets tired; he won't kick you or tread on your dress; he will hold you as firmly as you like, and go as quickly or a slowly as you please;

he never gets giddy; and he is full of conversation. Come, speak up for yourself, my boy."

'The old gentleman twisted one of the buttons at the back of his coat, and immediately Fritz opened his mouth, and in thin tones that appeared to proceed from the back of his head, remarked suddenly, "May I have the pleasure?" and then shut his mouth again with a snap.

'That Lieutenant Fritz had made a strong impression on the company was undoubted, yet none of the girls seemed inclined to dance with him. They looked askance at his waxen face, with its staring eyes and fixed smile, and shuddered. At last old Geibel came to the girl who had conceived the idea.

'"It is your own suggestion, carried out to the letter," said Geibel, "an electric dancer. You owe it to the gentleman to give him a trial."

'She was a bright, saucy little girl, fond of a frolic. Her host added his entreaties, and she consented.

'Herr Geibel fixed the figure to her. Its right arm was screwed round her waist, and held her firmly; its delicately jointed left hand was made to fasten upon her right. The old toymaker showed her how to regulate its speed, and how to stop it, and release herself.

'"It will take you round in a complete circle," he explained; "be careful that no one knocks against you, and alters its course."

'The music struck up. Old Geibel put the current in motion, and Annette and her strange partner began to dance.

'For a while everyone stood watching them. The figure performed its purpose admirably. Keeping perfect time and step, and holding its little partner tight clasped in an unyielding embrace, it revolved steadily, pouring forth at the same time a constant flow of squeaky conversation, broken by brief intervals of grinding silence.

'"How charming you are looking tonight," it remarked in its thin, far-away voice. "What a lovely day it has been. Do you like dancing? How well our steps agree. You will give me another, won't you? Oh, don't be so cruel. What a charming gown you have on. Isn't waltzing delightful? I could go on dancing for ever—with you. Have you had supper?"

'As she grew more familiar with the uncanny creature, the girl's nervousness wore off, and she entered into the fun of the thing.

'"Oh, he's just lovely," she cried, laughing; "I could go on dancing with him all my life."

'Couple after couple now joined them, and soon all the dancers in the room were whirling round behind them. Nicholaus Geibel stood looking on, beaming with childish delight at his success.

'Old Wenzel approached him, and whispered something in his ear. Geibel laughed and nodded, and the two worked their way quietly towards the door.

'"This is the young people's house tonight," said Wenzel, as soon as they were outside; "you and I will have a quiet pipe and glass of hock, over in the counting-house."

'Meanwhile, the dancing grew more fast and furious. Little Annette loosened the screw regulating her partner's rate of progress, and the figure flew round with her swifter and swifter. Couple after couple dropped out exhausted, but they only went the faster, till at length they remained dancing alone.

'Madder and madder became the waltz. The music lagged behind: the musicians, unable to keep pace, ceased, and sat staring. The younger guests applauded, but the older faces began to grow anxious.

'"Hadn't you better stop, dear," said one of the women, "you'll make yourself so tired."

'But Annette did not answer.

'"I believe she's fainted," cried out a girl who had caught sight of her face as it was swept by.

'One of the men sprang forward and clutched at the figure, but its impetus threw him down on to the floor, where its steel-cased feet laid bare his cheek. The thing evidently did not intend to part with its prize so easily.

'Had any one retained a cool head, the figure, one cannot help thinking, might easily have been stopped. Two or three men acting in concert might have lifted it bodily off the floor, or have jammed it into a corner. But few human heads are capable of remaining cool under excitement. Those who are not present think how stupid must have been those who were; those who are reflect afterwards how simple it would have been to do this, that, or the other, if only they had thought of it at the time.

'The women grew hysterical. The men shouted contradictory directions to one another. Two of them made a bungling rush at the figure, which had the end result of forcing it out of its orbit at the centre of the room, and sending it crashing against the walls and furniture. A stream of blood showed itself down the girl's white frock, and followed her along the floor. The affair was becoming horrible. The women rushed screaming from the room. The men followed them.

'One sensible suggestion was made: "Find Geibel—fetch Geibel."

'No one had noticed him leave the room, no one knew where he was. A party went in search of him. The others, too unnerved to go back into the ballroom, crowded outside the door and listened. They could hear the steady whir of the wheels upon the polished floor as the thing spun round and round; the dull thud as every now and again it dashed itself and its burden against some opposing object and ricocheted off in a new direction.

'And everlastingly it talked in that thin ghostly voice, repeating over and over the same formula: "How charming you look tonight. What a lovely day it has been. Oh, don't be so cruel. I could go on dancing for ever—with you. Have you had supper?"

'Of course they sought Geibel everywhere but where he was. They looked in every room in the house, then they rushed off in a body to his own place, and spent precious minutes waking up his deaf old housekeeper. At last it occurred to one of the party that Wenzel was missing also, and then the idea of the counting-house across the yard presented itself to them, and there they found him.

'He rose up, very pale, and followed them; and he and old Wenzel forced their way through the crowd of guests gathered outside, and entered the room, and locked the door behind them.

'From within there came the muffled sound of low voices and quick steps, followed by a confused scuffling noise, then silence, then the low voices again.

'After a time the door opened, and those near it pressed

forward to enter, but old Wenzel's broad head and shoulders barred the way.

'"I want you—and you, Bekler," he said, addressing a couple of the elder men. His voice was calm, but his face was deadly white. "The rest of you, please go—get the women away as quickly as you can."

'From that day old Nicholaus Geibel confined himself to the making of mechanical rabbits, and cats that mewed and washed their faces.'

The Man with the Cough

Mrs Molesworth

I am a German by birth and descent. My name is Schmidt. But by education I am quite as much an Englishman as a 'Deutscher,' and by affection much more the former. My life has been spent pretty equally between the two countries, and I flatter myself I speak both languages without any foreign accent.

I count England my headquarters now: it is 'home' to me. But a few years ago I was residing in Germany, only going over to London now and then on business. I will not mention the town where I lived. it is unnecessary to do so, and in the peculiar experience I am about to relate I think real names of people and places are just as well, or better, avoided.

I was connected with a large and important firm of engineers. I had been bred up to the profession, and was credited with a certain amount of talent; and I was considered—and, with all modesty, I think I deserved the opinion—steady and reliable, so that I had already attained a fair position in the house, and was looked upon as a 'rising man'. But I was still young, and not quite so wise as I thought myself. I came very near once to making a great mess of a certain affair. It is this story which I am going to tell.

Our house went in largely for patents—rather too largely, some thought. But the head partner's son was a bit of a genius in his way, and his father was growing old, and let Herr Wilhelm— Moritz we will call the family name—do pretty much as he chose. And on the whole Herr Wilhelm did well. He was cautious, and he had the benefit of the still greater caution and larger experience of Herr Gerhardt, the second partner in the firm.

Patents and the laws which regulate them are queer things to have to do with. No one who has not had personal experience of the complications that arise could believe how far these spread and how entangled they become. Great acuteness as well as caution is called for if you would guide your patent bark safely to port—and perhaps more than anything, a power of holding your tongue. I was no chatterbox, nor, when on a mission of importance, did I go about looking as if I were bursting with secrets, which is, in my opinion, almost as dangerous as revealing them. No one, to meet me on the journeys which it often fell to my lot to undertake, would have guessed that I had anything on my mind but an easy-going young fellow's natural interest in his surroundings, though many a time I have stayed awake through a whole night of railway travel if at all doubtful about my fellow-passengers, or not dared to go to sleep in a hotel without a ready-loaded revolver by my pillow.

For now and then—though not through me—our secrets did ooze out. And if, as *has* happened, they were secrets connected with government orders or contracts, there was, or but for the exertion of the greatest energy and tact on the part of my superiors, there *would* have been, to put it plainly, the devil to pay.

One morning—it was nearing the end of November—I was sent for to Herr Wilhelm's private room. There I found him and Herr Gerhardt before a table spread with papers covered with figures and calculations, and sheets of beautifully executed diagrams.

'Lutz,' said Herr Wilhelm. He had known me from childhood, and often called me by the abbreviation of my Christian name, which is Ludwig, or Louis. 'Lutz, we are going to confide to you a matter of extreme importance. You must be prepared to start for London tomorrow.'

'All right, sir,' I said, 'I shall be ready.'

'You will take the express through to Calais—on the whole it is the best route, especially at this season. By travelling all night you will catch the boat there, and arrive in London so as to have a good night's rest, and be clear-headed for work the next morning.'

I bowed agreement, but ventured to make a suggestion.

'If, as I infer, the matter is one of great importance,' I said, 'would it not be well for me to start sooner? I can—yes,' throwing a rapid survey over the work I had before me for the next two days—'I can be ready tonight.'

Herr Wilhelm looked at Herr Gerhardt. Herr Gerhardt shook his head.

'No,' he replied; 'tomorrow it must be,' and then he proceeded to explain to me why.

I need not attempt to give all the details of the matter with which I was entrusted. Indeed, to 'lay' readers it would be impossible. Suffice it to say, the whole concerned a patent—

that of a very remarkable and wonderful invention, which it was hoped and believed the governments of both countries would take up. But to secure this being done in a thoroughly satisfactory manner it was necessary that our firm should go about it in concert with an English house of first-rate standing. To this house—the firm of Messrs Bluestone and Fagg I will call them—I was to be sent with full explanations. And the next half-hour or more passed in my superiors going minutely into the details, so as to satisfy themselves that I understood. The mastering of the whole was not difficult, for I was well grounded technically; and like many of the best things the idea was essentially simple, and the diagrams were perfect. When the explanations were over, and my instructions duly noted, I began to gather together the various sheets, which were all numbered. But, to my surprise, Herr Gerhardt, looking over me, withdrew two of the most important diagrams, without which the others were valueless, because inexplicable.

'Stay,' he said; 'these two, Ludwig, must be kept separate. These we send today, by registered post, direct to Bluestone and Fagg. They will receive them a day before they see you, and with them a letter announcing your arrival.'

I looked up in some disappointment. I had known of precautions of the kind being taken, but usually when the employee sent was less reliable than I believed myself to be.

Still, I scarcely dared to demur.

'Do you think that necessary?' I said respectfully. 'I can assure you that from the moment you entrust me with the papers they shall never quit me day or night. And if there were any postal delay—you say time is valuable in this case—or if the papers were stolen in the transit—such things have happened—my whole mission would be worthless.'

'We do not doubt your zeal and discretion, my good Schmidt,' said Herr Gerhardt. 'But in this case we must take even extra precautions. I had not meant to tell you, fearing to add to the certain amount of nervousness and strain unavoidable in such a case, but still, perhaps it is best that you should know that we *have* reason for some special anxiety. It has been hinted to us that some breath of this'—and he tapped the papers—'has reached those who are always on the watch for such things. We cannot be too careful.'

'And yet,' I persisted, 'you would trust the post?'

'We do not trust the post,' he replied. 'Even if these diagrams were tampered with, they would be perfectly useless. And tampered with they will not be. But even supposing anything so wild, the rogues in question knowing of your departure (and they are *more* likely to know of it than of our packet by post), were they in collusion with some traitor in the post-office, are sharp enough to guess the truth—that we have made a Masonic secret of it—the two separate diagrams are valueless without your papers; *your* papers reveal nothing without nos. 7 and 13.'

I bowed in submission. But I was, all the same, disappointed, as I said, and a trifle mortified.

Herr Wilhelm saw it, and cheered me up.

'All right, Lutz, my boy,' he said. 'I feel just like you—nothing I should enjoy more than a rush over to London, carrying the whole documents, and prepared for a fight with any one who tried to get hold of them. But Herr Gerhardt here is cooler-blooded than we are.'

The elder man smiled.

'I don't doubt your readiness to fight, nor Ludwig's either. But it would be by no such honestly brutal means as open robbery that we should be outwitted. Make friends readily with no one while travelling, Lutz, yet avoid the appearance of keeping yourself aloof. You understand?'

'Perfectly,' I said. 'I shall sleep well tonight, so as to be prepared to keep awake throughout the journey.'

The papers were then carefully packed up. Those consigned to my care were to be carried in a certain light, black handbag with a very good lock, which had often before been my travelling companion.

And the following evening I started by the express train agreed upon. So, at least, I have always believed, but I have never been able to bring forward a witness to the fact of my train at the start being the right one, as no one came with me to see me off. For it was thought best that I should depart in as unobtrusive a manner as possible, as, even in a large town such as ours, the members and employees of an old and important house like the Moritzes' were well known.

I took my ticket then, registering no luggage, as I had none but what I easily carried in my hand, as well as *the* bag. It was already dusk, if not dark, and there was not much bustle in the station, nor apparently many passengers. I took my place in an empty second-class compartment, and sat there quietly till the train should start. A few minutes before it did so, another man got in. I was somewhat annoyed at this, as in my circumstances nothing was more undesirable than travelling alone with one other. Had there been a crowded compartment, or one with three or four passengers, I would have chosen it; but at the moment I got in, the carriages were all either empty or with but one or two occupants. Now, I said to myself, I should have done better to wait till nearer the time of departure, and then chosen my place.

I turned to reconnoitre my companion, but I could not see his face clearly, as he was half leaning out of the window. Was he doing so on purpose? I said to myself, for naturally I was in a suspicious mood. And as the thought struck me I half started up, determined to choose another compartment. Suddenly a peculiar sound made itself heard. My companion was coughing. He drew his head in, covering his face with his hand, as he coughed again. You never heard such a curious cough. It was more like a hen clucking than anything I can think of. Once, twice he coughed; then, as if he had been waiting for the slight spasm to pass, he sprang up, looked eagerly out of the window again, and, opening the door, jumped out, with some exclamation, as if he had just caught sight of a friend.

And in another moment or two—he could barely have had time to get in elsewhere—much to my satisfaction, the train moved off.

'Now,' thought I, 'I can make myself comfortable for some hours. We do not stop till M—: it will be nine o'clock by then. if no one gets in there I am safe to go through till tomorrow alone; then there will only be—Junction, and a clear run to Calais.'

I unstrapped my rug and lit a cigar—of course I had chosen a smoking-carriage—and, delighted at having got rid of my clucking companion, the time passed pleasantly till we pulled up at M—.The delay there was not great, and to my enormous satisfaction no one molested my solitude. Evidently the express to Calais was not in very great demand that night. I now felt so secure that, notwithstanding my intention of keeping awake all night, my innermost consciousness had not I suppose quite resigned itself to the necessity, for, not more than a hour or so after leaving M—, possibly sooner, I fell fast asleep.

It seemed to me that I had slept heavily, for when I awoke I had great difficulty in remembering where I was. Only by slow degrees did I realize that I was not in my comfortable bed at home, but in a chilly, ill-lighted railway- carriage. Chilly— yes, that it was—very chilly; but as my faculties returned I remembered my precious bag, and forgot all else in a momentary terror that it had been taken from me. No; there it was—my elbow had been pressed against it as I slept. But how was this? The train was not in motion. We were standing in a station; a dingy deserted-looking place, with no cheerful noise or bustle; only one or two porters slowly moving about, with a sort of sleepy 'night duty,' surly air. It could not be the Junction? I looked at my watch. Barely midnight! Of course, not the Junction. We were not due there till four o'clock in the morning or so.

What, then, were we doing here, and what *was* 'here'? Had there been an accident—some unforeseen necessity for stopping? At that moment a curious sound, from some yards' distance only it seemed to come, caught my ear. It was that croaking, cackling cough!—the cough of my momentary fellow passenger, towards whom I had felt an instinctive aversion. I looked out of the window—there was a refreshment-room just opposite, dimly lighted, like everything else, and in the doorway, as if just entering, was a figure which I felt pretty sure was that of the man with the cough.

'Bah!' I said to myself, 'I must not be fanciful. I dare say the fellow's all right. He is evidently in the same hole as myself. What in Heaven's name are we waiting here for?'

I sprang out of the carriage, nearly tumbling over a porter slowly passing along.

'How long are we to stay here?' I cried. 'When do we start again for—?' and I named the Junction.

'For—' he repeated in the queerest German I ever heard—was it German? or did I discover his meaning by some preternatural cleverness of my own? 'There is no train for—for four or five hours, not till—' and he named the time; and leaning forward lazily, he took out my larger bag and my rug, depositing them on the platform. He did not seem the least surprised at finding me there—I might have been there for a week, it seemed to me.

'No train for five hours? Are you mad?' I said.

He shook his head and mumbled something, and it seemed to me that he pointed to the refreshment-room opposite. Gathering my things together I hurried thither, hoping to find some more reliable authority. But there was no one there except a fat man with a white apron, who was clearing the counter— and—yes, in one corner was the figure I had mentally dubbed 'The man with the cough'.

I addressed the cook or waiter—whichever he was. But he only shook his head—denied all knowledge of the trains, but informed me that—in other words—I must turn out; he was going to shut up.

'And where am I to spend the night, then?' I said angrily,

though clearly it was not the aproned individual who was responsible for the position in which I found myself.

There was a 'Restauration', he informed me, near at hand, which I should find still open, straight before me on leaving the station, and then a few doors to the right, I would see the lights.

Clearly there was nothing else to be done. I went out, and as I did so the silent figure in the corner rose also and followed me. The station was evidently going to bed. As I passed the porter I repeated the hour he had named, adding: 'That is the first train for—Junction?'

He nodded, again naming the exact time. But I cannot do so, as I have never been able to recollect it.

I trudged along the road—there were lamps, though very feeble ones; but by their light I saw that the man who had been in the refreshment-room was still a few steps behind me. It made me feel slightly nervous, and I looked round furtively once or twice; the last time I did so he was not to be seen, and I hoped he had gone some other way.

The 'Restauration' was scarcely more inviting than the station refreshment-room. It, too, was very dimly lighted, and the one or two attendants seemed half asleep and were strangely silent. There was a fire, of a kind, and I seated myself at a small table near it and asked for some coffee, which would, I thought, serve the double purpose of warming me and keeping me awake.

It was brought to me, in silence. I drank it, and felt the better for it. But there was something so gloomy and unsociable, so queer and almost weird about the whole aspect and feeling of the place, that a sort of irritable resignation took possession of me. If these surly folks won't speak, neither will I, I said to myself childishly. And, incredible as it may sound, I did *not* speak. I think I paid for the coffee, but I am not quite sure. I know I never asked what I had meant to ask—the name of the town—a place of some importance, to judge by the size of the station and the extent of twinkling lights I had observed as I made my way to the 'Restauration'. From that day to this I have never been able to identify it, and I am quite sure I never shall.

What was peculiar about that coffee? Or was it something peculiar about my own condition that caused it to have the unusual effect I now experienced? That question, too, I cannot answer. All I remember is feeling a sensation of irresistible drowsiness creeping over me—mental, or moral I may say, as well as physical. For when one part of me feebly resisted the first onslaught of sleep, something seemed to reply: 'Oh, nonsense! you have several hours before you. Your papers are all right. No one can touch them without awaking you.'

And dreamily conscious that my belongings were on the floor at my feet—*the* bag itself actually resting against my ankle—my scruples silenced themselves in an extraordinary way. I remember nothing more, save a vague consciousness through all my slumber of confused and chaotic dreams, which I have never been able to recall.

I awoke at last, and that with a start, almost a jerk. Something had awakened me—a sound—and as it was repeated to my now aroused ears I knew that I had heard it before, off and on, during my sleep. It was the extraordinary cough!

I looked up. Yes, there he was! At some two or three yards' distance only, at the other side of the fireplace, which, and this

I have forgotten to mention as another peculiar item in that night's peculiar experiences, considering I have every reason to believe I was still in Germany, was not a stove, but an open grate.

And he had not been there when I first fell asleep; to that I was prepared to swear.

'He must have come sneaking in after me,' I thought, and in all probability I should neither have noticed nor recognized him but for that traitorous cackle of his.

Now, my misgivings aroused, my first thought, of course, was for my precious charge. I stooped. There were my rugs, my larger bag, but—no, not the smaller one; and though the other two were there, I knew at once that they were not quite in the same position—not so close to me. Horror seized me. Half wildly I gazed around, when my silent neighbour bent towards me. I could declare there was nothing in his hand when he did so, and I could declare as positively that I had already looked under the small round table beside which I sat, and that the bag was not there. And yet when the man, with a slight cackle, caused, no doubt, by his stooping, raised himself, the thing was in his hand!

Was he a conjurer, a pupil of Maskelyne and Cook? And how was it that, even as he held out my missing property, he managed, and that most cleverly and unobtrusively, to prevent my catching sight of his face? I did not see it then—I never did see it!

Something he murmured, to the effect that he supposed the bag was what I was looking for. In what language he spoke I know not; it was more that by the action accompanying the mumbled sounds I gathered his meaning, than that I heard anything articulate.

I thanked him, of course, mechanically, so to say, though I began to feel as if he were an evil spirit haunting me. I could only hope that the splendid lock to the bag had defied all curiosity, but I felt in a fever to be alone again, and able to satisfy myself that nothing had been tampered with.

The thought recalled my wandering faculties. How long had I been asleep? I drew out my watch. Heavens! It was close upon the hour named for the first train in the morning. I sprang up, collected my things, and dashed out of the 'Restauration'. If I had not paid for my coffee before, I certainly did not pay for it then. Besides my haste, there was another reason for this— there was no one to pay to! Not a creature was to be seen in the room or at the door as I passed out—always excepting the man with the cough.

As I left the place and hurried along the road, a bell began, not to ring, but to toll. It sounded most uncanny. What it meant, of course, I have never known. It may have been a summons to the work people of some manufactory, it may have been like all the other experiences of that strange night. But no; this theory I will not at present enter upon.

Dawn was not yet breaking, but there was in one direction a faint suggestion of something of the kind not far off. Otherwise all was dark. I stumbled along as best as I could, helped in reality, I suppose, by the ugly yellow glimmer of the woebegone street, or road lamps. And it was not far to the station, though somehow it seemed farther than when I came; and somehow, too, it seemed to have grown steep, though I could not remember having noticed any slope the other way on my arrival. A nightmare-like sensation began to oppress me. I felt as if my luggage was growing momentarily heavier and heavier, as if I should *never* reach the station; and to this was joined the agonizing terror of missing the train.

I made a desperate effort. Cold as it was, the beads of perspiration stood out upon my forehead as I forced myself along. And by degrees the nightmare feeling cleared off. I found myself entering the station at a run just as—yes, a train was actually beginning to move! I dashed, baggage and all, into a compartment; it was empty, and it was a second-class one, precisely similar to the one I had occupied before; it might have been the very same one. The train gradually increased its speed, but for the first few moments, while still in the station and passing through its immediate *entourage*, another strange thing struck me—the extraordinary silence and lifelessness of all about. Not one human being did I see, no porter watching our departure with the faithful though stolid interest always to be seen on the porter's visage. I might have been alone in the train—it might have had a freight of the dead, and been itself propelled by some supernatural agency, so noiselessly, so gloomily did it proceed.

You will scarcely credit that I actually and for the third time fell asleep. I could not help it. Some occult influence was at work upon me throughout those dark hours, I am positively certain. And with the daylight it was dispelled. For when I again awoke I felt for the first time since leaving home completely and normally myself, fresh and vigorous, all my faculties at their best.

But, nevertheless, my first sensation was a start of amazement, almost of terror. The compartment was nearly full! There were at least five or six travellers besides myself, very respectable, ordinary-looking folk, with nothing in the least alarming about them. Yet it was with a gasp of extraordinary relief that I found my precious bag in the corner beside me, where I had carefully placed it. It was concealed from view. No one, I felt assured, could have touched it without awaking me. It was broad and bright daylight. How long had I slept?

'Can you tell me,' I inquired of my opposite neighbour, a cheery-faced compatriot—'Can you tell me how soon we get to—Junction by this train? I am most anxious to catch the evening mail at Calais, and am quite out in my reckonings, owing to an extraordinary delay at—. I have wasted the night by getting into a stopping train instead of the express.'

He looked at me in astonishment. He must have thought me either mad or just awaking from a fit of intoxication—only I flatter myself I did not look as if the latter were the case.

'How soon we get to—Junction?' he repeated. 'Why, my good sir, you left it about three hours ago! It is now eight o'clock. We all got in at the Junction. You were alone, if I mistake not?'—he glanced at one or two of the others, who endorsed his statement. 'And very fast asleep you were, and must have been, not to be disturbed by the bustle at the station. And as for catching the evening boat at Calais'—he burst into a loud guffaw—'why, it would be very hard lines to do no better than that! We all hope to cross by the mid-day one.'

'Then—what train *is* this?' I exclaimed, utterly perplexed.

'The express, of course. All of us, excepting yourself, joined it at the Junction,' he replied. 'The express?' I repeated.

'The express that leaves'—and I named my own town—'at six in the evening?'

'Exactly. You have got into the right train after all,' and here came another shout of amusement. 'How did you think we had all got in if you had not yet passed the Junction? You had not the pleasure of our company from M—, I take it? M—, which you passed at nine o'clock last night, if my memory is correct.'

'Then,' I persisted, 'this is the double-fast express, which does not stop between M—and your Junction?'

'Exactly,' he repeated; and then, confirmed most probably in his belief that I was mad, or the other thing, he turned to his newspaper, and left me to my extraordinary cogitations.

Had I been dreaming? Impossible! Every sensation, the very taste of the coffee, seemed still present with me—the curious accent of the officials at the mysterious town, I could perfectly recall. I still shivered at the remembrance of the chilly waking in the 'Restauration'; I heard again the cackling cough.

But I felt I must collect myself, and be ready for the important negotiation entrusted to me. And to do this I must for the time banish these fruitless efforts at solving the problem.

We had a good run to Calais, found the boat in waiting, and a fair passage brought us prosperously across the Channel. I found myself in London punctual to the intended hour of my arrival.

At once I drove to the lodgings in a small street off the Strand which I was accustomed to frequent in such circumstances. I felt nervous till I had an opportunity of thoroughly overhauling my documents. The bag had been opened by the Custom House officials, but the words 'private papers' had sufficed to prevent any further examination; and to my unspeakable delight they were intact. A glance satisfied me as to this the moment I got them out, for they were most carefully numbered.

The next morning saw me early on my way to—No. 909, we will say—Blackfriars Street, where was the office of Messrs Bluestone & Fagg. I had never been there before, but it was easy to find, and had I felt any doubt, their name stared me in the face at the side of the open doorway. 'Second-floor' I thought I read; but when I reached the first landing I imagined I must have been mistaken. For there, at a door ajar, stood an eminently respectable-looking gentleman, who bowed as he saw me, with a discreet smile.

'Herr Schmidt?' he said. 'Ah, yes; I was on the look-out for you.'

I felt a little surprised, and my glance involuntarily strayed to the doorway. There was no name upon it, and it appeared to have been freshly painted. My new friend saw my glance.

'It is all right,' he said; 'we have the painters here. We are using these lower rooms temporarily. I was watching to prevent you having the trouble of mounting to the second-floor.'

And as I followed him in, I caught sight of a painter's ladder—a small one—on the stair above, and the smell was also unmistakable.

The large outer office looked bare and empty, but under the circumstances that was natural. No one was, at the first glance, to be seen; but behind a dulled glass partition screening off one corner I fancied I caught sight of a seated figure. And an inner office, to which my conductor led the way, had a more comfortable and inhabited look. Here stood a younger man. He bowed politely.

'Mr Fagg, my junior,' said the first individual airily. 'And now, Herr Schmidt, to business at once, if you please. Time is everything. You have all the documents ready?'

I answered by opening my bag and spreading out its contents. Both men were very grave, almost taciturn; but as I proceeded to explain things it was easy to see that they thoroughly understood all I said.

'And now,' I went on, when I had reached a certain point, 'if you will give me Nos. 7 and 13 which you have already received by registered post, I can put you in full possession of the whole. Without them, of course, all I have said is, so to say, preliminary only.'

The two looked at each other.

'Of course,' said the elder man, 'I follow what you say. The key of the whole is wanting. But I was momentarily expecting you to bring it out. We have not—Fagg, I am right, am I not— we have received nothing by post?'

'Nothing whatever,' replied his junior. And the answer seemed simplicity itself. Why did a strange thrill of misgiving go through me? Was it something in the look that had passed between them? Perhaps so. In any case, strange to say, the inconsistency between their having received no papers and yet looking for my arrival at the hour mentioned in the letter accompanying the documents, and accosting me by name, did not strike me till some hours later.

I threw off what I believed to be my ridiculous mistrust, and it was not difficult to do so in my extreme annoyance.

'I cannot understand it,' I said. 'It is really too bad. Everything depends upon 7 and 13. I must telegraph at once for inquiries to be instituted at the post-office.'

'But your people must have duplicates,' said Fagg eagerly. 'These can be forwarded at once.'

'I hope so,' I said, though feeling strangely confused and worried.

'They must send them direct *here*,' he went on.

I did not at once answer. I was gathering my papers together.

'And in the meantime,' he proceeded, touching my bag, 'you had better leave *these* here. We will lock them up in the safe at once. It is better than carrying them about London.'

It certainly seemed so. I half laid down the bag on the table, but at that moment from the outer room a most peculiar sound caught my ears—a faint cackling cough! I *think* I concealed my start. I turned away as if considering Fagg's suggestion, which, to confess the truth, I had been on the very point of agreeing to. For it would have been a great relief to me to know that the papers were in safe custody. But now a flash of lurid light seemed to have transformed everything.

'I thank you,' I replied. 'I should be glad to be free from the responsibility of the charge, but I dare not let these out of my own hands till the agreement is formally signed.'

The younger man's face darkened. He assumed a bullying tone.

'I don't know how it strikes *you*, Mr Bluestone,' he said, 'but it seems to me that this young gentleman is going rather too far. Do you think your employers will be pleased to hear of your insulting us, sir?'

But the elder man smiled condescendingly, though with a touch of superciliousness. It was very well done. He waved his hand.

'Stay, my dear Mr Fagg; we can well afford to make allowance. You will telegraph at once, no doubt, Herr Schmidt, and—let me see—yes, we shall receive the duplicates of Nos. 7 and 13 by first post on Thursday morning.'

I bowed.

'Exactly,' I replied, as I lifted the now locked bag. 'And you may expect me at the same hour on Thursday morning.'

Then I took my departure, accompanied to the door by the urbane individual who had received me.

The telegram which I at once despatched was not couched precisely as he would have dictated, I allow. And he would have been considerably surprised at my sending off another, later in the day, to Bluestone & Fagg's telegraphic address, in these words:

'Unavoidably detained till Thursday morning.—Schmidt.'

This was *after* the arrival of a wire from home in answer to mine.

By Thursday morning I had had time to receive a letter from Herr Wilhelm, and to secure the services of a certain noted detective, accompanied by whom I presented myself at the appointed hour at 909. But my companion's services were not required. The birds had flown, warned by the same traitor in our camp through whom the first hints of the new patent had leaked out. With him it was easy to deal, poor wretch! but the clever rogues who had employed him and personated the members of the honourable firm of Bluestone & Fagg were never traced.

The negotiation was successfully carried out. The experience I had gone through left me a wiser man. It is to be hoped, too, that the owners of 909 Blackfriars Street were more cautious in the future as to whom they let their premises to when temporarily vacant. The re-painting of the doorway, etc., at the tenant's own expense had already roused some slight suspicion.

It is needless to add that Nos. 7 and 13 had been duly received on the second-floor.

I have never known the true history of that extraordinary night. Was it all a dream, or a prophetic vision of warning? Or was it in any sense true? *Had* I, in some inexplicable way, left my own town earlier than I intended, and really travelled in a slow train?

Or had the man with a cough, for his own nefarious purposes, mesmerized or hypnotized me, and to some extent succeeded?

I cannot say. Sometimes, even, I ask myself if I am quite sure that there ever was such a person as 'the man with the cough'!

Laura

Saki

'You are not really dying, are you?' asked Amanda.

'I have the doctor's permission to live till Tuesday,' said Laura.

'But today is Saturday; this is serious!' gasped Amanda.

'I don't know about it being serious; it is certainly Saturday,' said Laura.

'Death is always serious,' said Amanda.

'I never said I was going to die. I am presumably going to leave off being Laura, but I shall go on being something. An animal of some kind, I suppose. You see, when one hasn't been very good in the life one has just lived, one reincarnates in some lower organism. And I haven't been very good, when one comes to think of it. I've been petty and mean and vindictive and all that sort of thing when circumstances have seemed to warrant it.'

'Circumstances never warrant that sort of thing,' said Amanda hastily.

'If you don't mind my saying so,' observed Laura, 'Egbert

is a circumstance that would warrant any amount of that sort of thing. You're married to him—that's different; you've sworn to love, honour, and endure him: I haven't.'

'I don't see what's wrong with Egbert,' protested Amanda.

'Oh, I dare say the wrongness has been on my part,' admitted Laura dispassionately; 'he has merely been the extenuating circumstance. He made a thin, peevish kind of fuss, for instance, when I took the collie puppies from the farm out for a run the other day.'

'They chased his young broods of speckled Sussex and drove two sitting hens off their nests, besides running all over the flower beds. You know how devoted he is to his poultry and garden.'

'Anyhow, he needn't have gone on about it for the entire evening and then have said, "Let's say no more about it" just when I was beginning to enjoy the discussion. That's where one of my petty vindictive revenges came in,' added Laura with an unrepentant chuckle; 'I turned the entire family of speckled Sussex into his seedling shed the day after the puppy episode.'

'How could you?' exclaimed Amanda.

'It came quite easy,' said Laura; 'two of the hens pretended to be laying at the time, but I was firm.'

'And we thought it was an accident!'

'You see,' resumed Laura, 'I really *have* some grounds for supposing that my next incarnation will be in a lower organism. I shall be an animal of some kind. On the other hand, I haven't been a bad sort in my way, so I think I may count on being a nice animal, some thing elegant and lively, with a love of fun. An otter, perhaps.'

'I can't imagine you as an otter,' said Amanda. 'Well, I don't suppose you can imagine me as an angel, if it comes to that,' said Laura.

Amanda was silent. She couldn't.

'Personally I think an otter life would be rather enjoyable,' continued Laura; 'salmon to eat all the year around, and the satisfaction of being able to fetch the trout in their own homes without having to wait for hours till they condescend to rise to the fly you've been dangling before them; and an elegant svelte figure—'

'Think of the otter hounds,' interposed Amanda; 'how dreadful to be hunted and harried and finally worried to death!'

'Rather fun with half the neighbourhood looking on, and anyhow not worse than this Saturday-to-Tuesday business of dying by inches; and then I should go on into something else. If I had been a moderately good otter I suppose I should get back into human shape of some sort; probably something rather primitive—a little brown, unclothed Nubian boy, I should think.'

'I wish you would be serious,' sighed Amanda; 'you really ought to be if you're only going to live till Tuesday.'

As a matter of fact Laura died on Monday.

'So dreadfully upsetting,' Amanda complained to her uncle in-law, Sir Lulworth Quayne. 'I've asked quite a lot of people down for golf and fishing, and the rhododendrons are just looking their best.'

'Laura always was inconsiderate,' said Sir Lulworth; 'she was born during Goodwood week, with an ambassador staying in the house who hated babies.'

'She had the maddest kind of ideas,' said Amanda; 'do you

know if there was any insanity in her family?'

'Insanity? No, I never heard of any. Her father lives in West Kensington, but I believe he's sane on all other subjects.'

'She had an idea that she was going to be reincarnated as an otter,' said Amanda.

'One meets with those ideas of reincarnation so frequently, even in the West,' said Sir Lulworth, 'that one can hardly set them down as being mad. And Laura was such an unaccountable person in this life that I should not like to lay down definite rules as to what she might be doing in an after-state.'

'You think she really might have passed into some animal form?' asked Amanda. She was one of those who shape their opinions rather readily from the standpoint of those around them.

Just then Egbert entered the breakfast-room, wearing an air of bereavement that Laura's demise would have been insufficient, in itself, to account for.

'Four of my speckled Sussex have been killed,' he exclaimed; 'the very four that were to go to the show on Friday. One of them was dragged away and eaten right in the middle of that new carnation bed that I've been to such trouble and expense over. My best flowerbed and my best fowls singled out for destruction; it almost seems as if the brute that did the deed had special knowledge how to be as devastating as possible in a short space of time.'

'Was it a fox, do you think?' asked Amanda.

'Sounds more like a polecat,' said Sir Lulworth.

'No,' said Egbert, 'there were marks of webbed feet all over the place, and we followed the tracks down to the stream at the bottom of the garden; evidently an otter.'

Amanda looked quickly and furtively across at Sir Lulworth. Egbert was too agitated to eat any breakfast, and went out to superintend the strengthening of the poultry yard defences. I think she might at least have waited till the funeral was over,' said Amanda in a scandalized voice.

'It's her own funeral, you know,' said Sir Lulworth; 'it's a nice point in etiquette how far one ought to show respect to one's own mortal remains.'

Disregard for mortuary convention was carried to further lengths next day; during the absence of the family at the funeral ceremony the remaining survivors of the speckled Sussex were massacred. The marauder's line of retreat seemed to have embraced most of the flowerbeds on the lawn, but the strawberry beds in the lower garden had also suffered.

'I shall get the otter hounds to come here at the earliest possible moment,' said Egbert savagely.

'On no account! You can't dream of such a thing!' exclaimed Amanda. 'I mean, it wouldn't do, so soon after a funeral in the house.'

'It's a case of necessity,' said Egbert; 'once an otter takes to that sort of thing it won't stop.'

'Perhaps it will go elsewhere now that there are no more fowls left,' suggested Amanda.

'One would think you wanted to shield the beast,' said Egbert.

'There's been so little water in the stream lately,' objected Amanda; 'it seems hardly sporting to hunt an animal when it has so little chance of taking refuge anywhere.'

'Good gracious!' fumed Egbert, 'I'm not thinking about sport. I want to have the animal killed as soon as possible.'

Even Amanda's opposition weakened when, during church time on the following Sunday, the otter made its way into the house, raided half a salmon from the larder and worried it into scaly fragments on the Persian rug in Egbert's studio.

'We shall have it hiding under our beds and biting pieces out of our feet before long,' said Egbert, and from what Amanda knew of this particular otter she felt that the possibility was not a remote one.

On the evening preceding the day fixed for the hunt Amanda spent a solitary hour walking by the banks of the stream, making what she imagined to be hound noises. It was charitably supposed by those who overheard her performance, that she was practising for farmyard imitations at the forthcoming village entertainment.

It was her friend and neighbour, Aurora Burnet, who brought her news of the day's sport.

'Pity you weren't out; we had quite a good day. We found it at once, in the pool just below your garden.'

'Did you—kill?' asked Amanda.

'Rather. A fine she-otter. Your husband got rather badly bitten in trying to "tail it". Poor beast, I felt quite sorry for it, it had such a human look in its eyes when it was killed. You'll call me silly, but do you know who the look reminded me of? My dear woman, what is the matter?'

When Amanda had recovered to a certain extent from her attack of nervous prostration Egbert took her to the Nile Valley to recuperate. Change of scene speedily brought about the desired recovery of health and mental balance. The escapades of an adventurous otter in search of a variation of diet were viewed in their proper light. Amanda's normally placid temperament reasserted itself. Even a hurricane of shouted curses, coming from her husband's dressing-room, in her husband's voice, but hardly in his usual vocabulary, failed to disturb her serenity as she made a leisurely toilet one evening in a Cairo hotel.

'What is the matter? What has happened?' she asked in amused curiosity.

'The little beast has thrown all my clean shirts into the bath! Wait till I catch you, you little—'

'What little beast?' asked Amanda, suppressing a desire to laugh; Egbert's language was so hopelessly inadequate to express his outraged feelings.

'A little beast of a naked brown Nubian boy,' spluttered Egbert. And now Amanda is seriously ill.

The Great French Duel

Mark Twain

Much as the modern French duel is ridiculed by certain smart people, it is in reality one of the most dangerous institutions of our day. Since it is always fought in the open air the combatants are nearly sure to catch cold. M. Paul de Cassagnac, the most inveterate of the French duellists, has suffered so often in this way that he is at last a confirmed invalid; and the best physician in Paris has expressed the opinion that if he goes on dueling for fifteen or twenty years more—unless he forms the habit of fighting in a comfortable room where damps and draughts cannot intrude—he will eventually endanger his life. This ought to moderate the talk of those people who are so stubborn in maintaining that the French duel is the most health-giving of recreations because of the open-air exercise it affords. And it ought also to moderate that foolish talk about French duellists and socialist-hated monarchs being the only people who are immortal.

But it is time to get to my subject. As soon as I heard of the late fiery outbreak between M. Gambetta and M. Fourtou in the French assembly, I knew that trouble must follow. I knew it because a long personal friendship with M. Gambetta had revealed to me the desperate and implacable nature of the man. Vast as his physical proportion, I knew that the thirst for revenge would penetrate to the remotest frontiers of his person. I did not wait for him to call on me, but went at once to him. As I expected, I found the brave fellow steeped in a profound French calm. I say French, because French calmness and English calmness have points of difference. He was moving swiftly back and forth among the debris of his furniture, now and then staving chance fragments of it across the room with his foot; grinding a constant grist of curses through his set teeth; and halting every little while to deposit another handful of his hair on the pile which he had been building of it on the table.

He threw his arms around my neck, bent me over his stomach to his breast, kissed me on both cheeks, hugged me four or five times and then placed me in his own arm chair. As soon as I got well again, we began business at once.

I said I supposed he would wish me to act as his second, and he said, 'Of course.' I said I must be allowed to act under a French name, so that I might be shielded from obloquy in my country, in case of fatal result. He winced here, probably at the suggestion that duelling was not regarded with respect in America. However, he agreed to my requirement. This accounts for the fact that in all the newspaper reports M. Gambetta's second was apparently a Frenchman.

First, we drew up my principal's will. I insisted upon this, and stuck to my point. I said I never heard of a man in his right mind going out to fight a duel without first making his will.

He said he had never heard of a man in his right mind doing anything of the kind. When he had finished his will, he wished to proceed to a choice of 'last words'. He wanted to know how the following words, as a dying exclamation, struck me:

'I die for my God, for my country, for freedom of speech, for progress, and the universal brotherhood of man!'

I objected that this would require too lingering a death; it was a good speech for a consumptive, but not suited to the exigencies of the field of honour. We wrangled over a good many ante-mortem outburst, but I finally got him to cut his obituary down to this, which he copied into his memorandum book, purposing to get it by heart:

'I DIE THAT FRANCE MAY LIVE.'

I said that this remark seemed to lack relevancy; but he said relevancy was a matter of no consequence in last words—what you wanted was thrill.

The next thing in order was the choice of weapon. My principal said he was not feeling well, and would leave that and the other details of the proposed meeting to me. Therefore I wrote the following note and carried it to M. Fourtou's friend:

'Sir, M. Gambetta accepts M. Fourtou's challenge and authorizes me to propose Plessis-Piquet as the place of meeting; tomorrow morning at daybreak as the time; and axes as the weapons. I am, sir, with great respect, Mark Twain.'

M. Fourtou's friend read this note, and shuddered. Then he turned to me and said, with a suggestion of severity in his tone:

'Have you considered, sir, what would be the inevitable result of such a meeting as this?'

'Well, for instance, what *would* it be?'

'Bloodshed!'

'That's about the size of it,' I said. 'Now, if it is a fair question, what was your side proposing to shed?'

I had him there. He saw he had made a blunder, so he hastened to explain it away. He said he had spoken jestingly. Then he added that he and his principal would enjoy axes, and indeed prefer them, but such weapons were barred by the French code, and so I must change my proposal.

I walked the floor, turning the thing over in my mind, and finally it occurred to me that Gatling guns at fifteen paces would be a likely way to get a verdict on the field of honour. So I framed this idea into a proposition.

But it was not accepted. The code was in the way again. I proposed rifles; then double-barrelled shot-guns; then Colt's navy revolvers. These being all rejected, I reflected a while and sarcastically suggested brickbats at three-quarters of a mile. I always hate to fool away a humorous thing on a person who has no perception of humour; and it filled me with bitterness when this man went soberly away to submit this last proposition to his principal.

He came back presently and said his principal was charmed with the idea of brickbats at three-quarters of a mile, but must decline on account of the danger to disinterested parties passing between. Then I said:

'Well, I am at the end of my string now. Perhaps you would be good enough to suggest a weapon. Perhaps you have even had one in your mind all the time?'

'Oh, without doubt, monsieur!'

So he fell to hunting in his pocket—pocket after pocket, and he had plenty of them—muttering all the while, 'Now, what could I have done with them?'

At last he was successful. He fished out of his vest pocket a couple of little things which I carried to the light and ascertained to be pistols. They were single-barrelled and silver-mounted, and very dainty and pretty. I was not able to speak for emotion. I silently hung one of them on my watchchain, and returned the other. My companion-in-crime now unrolled a postage stamp containing several cartridges, and gave me one of them. I asked if he meant to signify by this that our men were to be allowed but one shot a piece. He replied that the French code permitted no more. I then begged him to go on and suggest a distance, for my mind was growing weak and confused under the strain which had been put upon it. He named sixty-five yards. I nearly lost my patience. I said:

'Sixty-five yards, with these instruments? Squirt guns would be deadlier at fifty. Consider, my friend, you and I are banded together to destroy life, not make it eternal.'

But with all my persuasions, all my arguments, I was only able to get him to reduce the distance to thirty-five yards; and even this concession he made with reluctance, and said with a sigh:

'I wash my hands of this slaughter; on your head be it.'

There was nothing for me but to go home to my old lion heart and tell my humiliating story. When I entered, M. Gambetta was laying his last lock of hair upon the altar. He sprang towards me, exclaiming:

'You have made the fatal arrangements—I see it in your eyes!'

'I have.'

His face paled a trifle, and he leaned upon a table for support. He breathed thick and heavily for a moment or two, so tumultuous were his feelings; then he hoarsely whispered:

'The weapon, the weapon! Quick! What is the weapon?'

'This!' and I displayed that silver-mounted thing. He cast but one glance at it, then swooned ponderously to the floor.

When he came to, he said mournfully:

'The unnatural calm to which I have subjected myself has told upon my nerves. But away with weakness! I will confront my fate like a man and a Frenchman.'

He rose to his feet, and assumed an attitude which for sublimity has never been approached by man, and had seldom been surpassed by statues. Then he said, in deep bass tones:

'Behold I am calm, I am ready, reveal to me the distance.'

'Thirty-five yards...'

I could not lift him up, of course; but I rolled him over, and poured water down his back. He presently came to, and said:

'Thirty-five yards—without a rest? But why ask? Since murder was that man's intention, why should he palter with small details? But mark you one thing: in my fall the world shall see how the chivalry of France meets death.'

At half-past nine in the morning the procession approached the field of Plessis-Piquet in the following order: first came our carriage—nobody in it but M. Gambetta and myself; then a carriage containing two poet-orators who did not believe in God, and these had MS funeral orations projecting from their breast pockets; then a carriage containing the head surgeons and their case of instruments; then eight private carriages containing consulting surgeons; then a hack containing a coroner; then two hearses; then a carriage containing the head undertakers; then a train of assistants and mutes on foot; and after these came plodding through the fog a long procession of camp followers, police, and citizens generally. It was a noble turnout, and would have made a fine display if we had thinner weather.

There was no conversation. I spoke several times to my principal, but I judge he was not aware of it, for he always referred to his notebook and muttered absently, 'I die that France may live.'

Arrived on the field, my fellow-second and I paced off the thirty-five yards, and then drew lots for choice of position. This latter was but an ornamental ceremony, for all choices were alike in such weather. These preliminaries being ended, I went to my principal and asked him if he was ready. He spread himself out to his full width, and said in stern voice, 'Ready! Let the batteries be charged.'

The loading was done in the presence of duly-constituted witnesses. We considered it best to perform this delicate service with the assistance of a lantern, on account of the state of the weather. We now placed our men.

At this point the police noticed that the public had massed themselves together on the right and left of the field; they therefore begged a delay, while they should put these poor people in a place of safety. The request was granted.

The police having ordered the two multitudes to take positions behind the duellists, we were once more ready. The weather growing still more opaque, it was agreed between myself and the other second that before giving the fatal signal

we should each deliver a loud whoop to enable the combatants
to ascertain each other's whereabouts.

I now returned to my principal, and was distressed to
observe that he had lost a good deal of his spirit. I tried my
best to hearten him. I said, 'Indeed, Sir, things are not as bad
as they seem. Considering the character of the weapons, the
limited number of shots allowed, the generous distance, the
impenetrable solidity of the fog, and the added fact that one of
the combatants is one-eyed and the other crossed-eyed and near-
sighted, it seems to be that this conflict need not necessarily be
fatal. There are chances that both of you may survive. Therefore
cheer up; do not be downhearted.' This speech had so good an
effect that my principal immediately stretched forth his hand
and said, 'I am myself again; give me the weapon.'

I laid it, all lonely and forlorn, in the centre of the vast
solitude of his palm. He gazed at it and shuddered. And still
mournfully contemplating it he murmured, in a broken voice:

'Alas! it is not death I dread, but mutilation.'

I heartened him once more, and with such success that he
presently said, 'Let the tragedy begin. Stand at my back; do not
desert me in this solemn hour, my friend.'

I gave him my promise. I now assisted him to point his
pistol towards the spot where I judged his adversary to be
standing, and cautioned him to listen well and further guide
himself by my fellow-second's whoop. Then I propped myself
against M. Gambetta's back, and raised a rousing 'Whoop-ee!'
This was answered from out the far distances of the fog, and
I immediately shouted:

'One-two-three-fire!'

Two little sounds like *spit! spit!* broke upon my ear, and in the same instant I was crushed to the earth under a mountain of flesh. Bruised as I was, I was still able to catch a faint accent from above, to this effect:

'I die for...for...perdition take it, what is it I die for? Oh, yes—FRANCE! I die that France may live!'

The surgeons swarmed around with their probes in their hands, and applied their microscopes to the whole area of M. Gambetta's person, with the happy result of finding nothing in the nature of a wound. Then a scene ensued which was in every way gratifying and inspiriting.

The two gladiators fell upon each other's necks, with floods of proud and happy tears; the other second embraced me; the surgeons, the orators, the undertakers, the police, everybody embraced, everybody congratulated, everybody cried, and the whole atmosphere was filled with praise and with joy unspeakable.

It seemed to me then that I would rather be a hero of a French duel than a crowned and sceptred monarch.

When the commotion had somewhat subsided, the body of surgeons held a consultation, and after a good deal of debate decided that with proper care and nursing there was reason to believe that I should survive my injuries. My internal hurts were deemed the most serious, since it was apparent that a broken rib had penetrated my left lung, and that many of my organs had been pressed out so far to one side or the other of where they belonged, that it was doubtful if they would ever learn to perform their functions in such remote and unaccustomed localities. They then set my arm in two places, pulled my right hip into its socket again, and re-elevated my nose. I was an object of great interest, and even administration; and many sincere and warm-hearted persons had themselves introduced to me, and said they were proud to know the only man who had been hurt in a French duel in forty years.

I was placed in an ambulance at the very head of the procession and thus with gratifying éclat I was marched into Paris, the most conspicuous figure in that great spectacle, and deposited at the hospital.

The Cross of the Legion of Honour has been conferred upon me. However, few escape that distinction.

Such is the true version of the most memorable private conflict of the age.

I lave no complaints to make against anyone. I acted for myself, and I can stand the consequences. Without boasting, I think I can say I am not afraid to stand before a modern French duellist, but as long as I keep in my right mind I will never consent to stand behind one again.

The Masque of the Red Death

Edgar Allan Poe

THE 'Red Death' had long devastated the country. No pestilence had ever been so fatal, or so hideous. Blood was its Avatar and its seal—the redness and the horror of blood. There were sharp pains, and sudden dizziness, and then profuse bleeding at the pores, with dissolution. The scarlet stains upon the body and especially upon the face of the victim, were the pest ban which shut him out from the aid and from the sympathy of his fellow-men. And the whole seizure, progress, and termination of the disease, were the incidents of half an hour.

But the Prince Prospero was happy and dauntless and sagacious. When his dominions were half depopulated, he summoned to his presence a thousand hale and light-hearted friends from among the knights and dames of his court, and with these retired to the deep seclusion of one of his castellated abbeys. This was an extensive and magnificent structure, the creation of the prince's own eccentric yet august taste. A strong and lofty wall girdled it in. This wall had gates of iron. The courtiers, having entered, brought furnaces and massy hammers and welded the bolts. They resolved to leave means neither of ingress nor egress to the sudden impulses of despair or of frenzy from within. The abbey was amply provisioned. With such precautions the courtiers might bid defiance to contagion. The external world could take care of itself. In the meantime it was folly to grieve, or to think. The prince had provided all the appliances of pleasure. There were buffoons, there were improvisator, there were ballet-dancers, there were musicians, there was beauty, there was wine. All these and security were within. Without was the 'Red Death'.

It was towards the close of the fifth or sixth month of his seclusion, and while the pestilence raged most furiously abroad, that the Prince Prospero entertained his thousand friends at a masked ball of the most unusual magnificence.

It was a voluptuous scene, that masquerade. But first let me tell of the rooms in which it was held. These were seven—an imperial suite. In many palaces, however, such suites form a long and straight vista, while the folding doors slide back nearly to the walls on either hand, so that the view of the whole extent is scarcely impeded. Here the case was very different, as might have been expected from the duke's love of the *bizarre*. The apartments were so irregularly disposed that the vision embraced but little more than one at a time. There was a sharp turn at every twenty or thirty yards, and at each turn a novel effect. To the right and left, in the middle of each wall, a tall and narrow Gothic window looked out upon a closed corridor which pursued the windings of the suite. These windows were of stained glass whose colour varied in accordance with the prevailing hue of the decorations of the chamber into which it opened. That at the eastern extremity was hung, for example, in blue—and vividly blue were its windows. The second chamber was purple in its ornaments and tapestries, and here the panes were purple. The third was green throughout, and so were the casements. The fourth was furnished and lighted with orange, the fifth with white and the sixth with violet. The seventh apartment was closely shrouded in black velvet tapestries that hung all over the ceiling and down the walls, falling in heavy folds upon a carpet of the same material and hue. But in this chamber only, the colour of the windows failed to correspond with the decorations. The panes here were scarlet—a deep blood colour. Now in no one of the seven apartments was there any lamp or candelabrum, amid the profusion of golden ornaments that lay scattered to and fro or depended from the roof. There was no light of any kind emanating from lamp or candle within the suite of chambers. But in the corridors that followed the suite, there stood, opposite to each window, a heavy tripod, bearing a brazier of fire, that projected its rays through the tinted glass and so glaringly illumined the room. And thus were produced a multitude of gaudy and fantastic appearances. But in the western or black chamber the effect of the firelight that streamed upon the dark hangings through the blood-tinted panes, was ghastly in the extreme, and produced so wild a look upon the countenances of those who entered, that there were few of the company bold enough to set foot within its precincts at all.

It was in this apartment, also, that there stood against the western wall, a gigantic clock of ebony. Its pendulum swung to and fro with a dull, heavy, monotonous clang; and when the minute-hand made the circuit of the face, and the hour was to be stricken, there came from the brazen lungs of the clock a sound which was clear and loud and deep and exceedingly musical, but of so peculiar a note and emphasis that, at each lapse of an hour, the musicians of the orchestra were constrained to pause, momentarily, in their performance, to hearken to the sound; and thus the waltzers perforce ceased their evolutions; and there was a brief disconcert of the whole gay company; and, while the chimes of the clock yet rang, it was observed that the giddiest grew pale, and the more aged and sedate passed their hands over their brows as if in confused reverie or meditation. But when the echoes had fully ceased, a light laughter at once pervaded the assembly; the musicians looked at each other and smiled as if at their own nervousness and folly, and made whispering vows, each to the other, that the next chiming of the clock should produce in them no similar emotion; and then, after the lapse of sixty minutes (which embrace three thousand and six hundred seconds of the Time that flies), there came yet another chiming of the clock, and then were the same disconcert and tremulousness and meditation as before.

But, in spite of these things, it was a gay and magnificent revel. The tastes of the duke were peculiar. He had a fine eye for colours and effects. He disregarded the *decora* of mere fashion. His plans were bold and fiery, and his conceptions glowed with barbaric lustre. There are some who would have thought him mad. His followers felt that he was not. It was necessary to hear and see and touch him to be *sure* that he was not.

He had directed, in great part, the movable embellishments

of the seven chambers, upon occasion of this great *fête*; and it was his own guiding taste which had given character to the masqueraders. Be sure they were grotesque. There were much glare and glitter and piquancy and phantasm—much of what has been since seen in 'Hernani'. There were arabesque figures with unsuited limbs and appointments. There were delirious fancies such as the madman fashions. There were much of the beautiful, much of the wanton, much of the *bizarre*, something of the terrible, and not a little of that which might have excited disgust. To and fro in the seven chambers there stalked, in fact, a multitude of dreams. And these—the dreams—writhed in and about, taking hue from the rooms, and causing the wild music of the orchestra to seem as the echo of their steps. And, anon, there strikes the ebony clock which stands in the hall of the velvet. And then, for a moment, all is still, and all is silent save the voice of the clock. The dreams are stiff—frozen as they stand. But the echoes of the chime die away—they have endured but an instant—and a light, half-subdued laughter floats after them as they depart. And now again the music swells, and the dreams live, and writhe to and fro more merrily than ever, taking hue from the many-tinted windows through which stream the rays from the tripods. But to the chamber which lies most westwardly of the seven, there are now none of the maskers who venture; for the night is waning away; and there flows a ruddier light through the blood-coloured panes; and the blackness of the sable drapery appalls; and to him whose foot falls upon the sable carpet, there comes from the near clock of ebony a muffled peal more solemnly emphatic than any which reaches *their* ears who indulge in the more remote gaieties of the other apartments.

But these other apartments were densely crowded, and in them beat feverishly the heart of life. And the revel went whirlingly on, until at length there commenced the sounding of midnight upon the clock. And then the music ceased, as I have told; and the evolutions of the waltzers were quieted; and there was an uneasy cessation of all things as before. But now there were twelve strokes to be sounded by the bell of the clock; and thus it happened, perhaps, that more of thought crept, with more of time, into the meditations of the thoughtful among those who revelled. And thus too, it happened, perhaps, that before the last echoes of the last chime had utterly sunk into silence, there were many individuals in the crowd who had found leisure to become aware of the presence of a masked figure which had arrested the attention of no single individual before. And the rumour of this new presence having spread itself whisperingly around, there arose at length from the whole company a buzz, or murmur, expressive of disapprobation and surprise—then, finally, of terror, of horror, and of disgust.

In an assembly of phantasms such as I have painted, it may well be supposed that no ordinary appearance could have excited such sensation. In truth the masquerade licence of the night was nearly unlimited; but the figure in question had out-Heroded Herod, and gone beyond the bounds of even the prince's indefinite decorum. There are chords in the hearts of the most reckless which cannot be touched without emotion. Even with the utterly lost, to whom life and death are equally jests, there are matters of which no jest can be made. The whole company, indeed, seemed now deeply to feel that in the costume and bearing of the stranger neither wit nor propriety existed.

The figure was tall and gaunt, and shrouded from head to foot in the habiliments of the grave. The mask which concealed the visage was made so nearly to resemble the countenance of a stiffened corpse that the closest scrutiny must have had difficulty in detecting the cheat. And yet all this might have been endured, if not approved, by the mad revellers around. But the mummer had gone so far as to assume the type of the Red Death. His vesture was dabbled in *blood*—and his broad brow, with all the features of the face, was besprinkled with the scarlet horror.

When the eyes of the Prince Prospero fell upon this spectral image (which, with a slow and solemn movement, as if more fully to sustain its role, stalked to and fro among the waltzers) he was seen to be convulsed, in the first moment with a strong shudder either of terror or distaste; but, in the next, his brow reddened with rage.

'Who dares'—he demanded hoarsely of the courtiers who stood near him—'who dares insult us with this blasphemous mockery? Seize him and unmask him—that we may know whom we have to hang, at sunrise, from the battlements!'

It was in the eastern or blue chamber in which stood the Prince Prospero as he uttered these words. They rang throughout the seven rooms loudly and clearly, for the prince was a bold and robust man, and the music had become hushed at the waving of his hand.

It was in the blue room where stood the prince, with a group of pale courtiers by his side. At first, as he spoke, there was a slight rushing movement of this group in the direction of the intruder, who, at the moment was also near at hand, and now, with deliberate and stately step, made closer approach to the speaker. But from a certain nameless awe with which the mad assumptions of the mummer had inspired the whole party, there were found none who put forth hand to seize him; so that, unimpeded, he passed within a yard of the prince's person; and, while the vast assembly, as if with one impulse, shrank from the centres of the rooms to the walls, he made his way uninterruptedly, but with the same solemn and measured step which had distinguished him from the first, through the blue chamber to the purple—through the purple to the green— through the green to the orange—through this again to the white—and even thence to the violet, ere a decided movement had been made to arrest him. It was then, however, that the Prince Prospero, maddening with rage and the shame of his own momentary cowardice, rushed hurriedly through the six chambers, while none followed him on account of a deadly terror that had seized upon all. He bore aloft a drawn dagger, and had approached, in rapid impetuosity, to within three or four feet of the retreating figure, when the latter, having attained the extremity of the velvet apartment, turned suddenly and confronted his pursuer. There was a sharp cry—and the dagger dropped gleaming upon the sable carpet, upon which, instantly afterward, fell prostrate in death the Prince Prospero. Then, summoning the wild courage of despair, a throng of the revellers at once threw themselves into the black apartment, and, seizing the mummer, whose tall figure stood erect and motionless within the shadow of the ebony clock, gasped in unutterable horror at finding the grave cerements and corpse-like mask, which they handled with so violent a rudeness, untenanted by any tangible form.

And now was acknowledged the presence of the Red Death. He had come like a thief in the night. And one by one dropped the revellers in the blood-bedewed halls of their revel, and died each in the despairing posture of his fall. And the life of the ebony clock went out with that of the last of the gay. And the flames of the tripods expired. And Darkness and Decay and the Red Death held illimitable dominion over all.

A Mussoorie Mystery

Ruskin Bond

Conan Doyle, the creator of Sherlock Holmes, had a lifelong interest in unusual criminal cases, and his friends often passed on to him interesting accounts of crime and detection from around the world. It was in this way that he learnt of the strange death of Miss Frances Garnett-Orme in the Indian hill-station of Mussoorie. Here was a murder combining the weird borders of the occult with a crime mystery as inexplicable as any devised by Doyle himself.

In April 1912 (shortly before the Titanic went down) Conan Doyle received a letter from his Sussex neighbour Rudyard Kipling:

Dear Doyle,
There has been a murder in India... A murder by suggestion at Mussoorie, which is one of the most curious things in its line on record.
Everything that is improbable and on the face of it impossible is in this case.

Kipling had received details of the case from a friend working in the Allahabad *Pioneer*, a paper for which, as a young man, he had worked in the 1880s. Urging Doyle to pursue the story, Kipling concluded: 'The psychology alone is beyond description.'

Doyle was indeed interested to hear more, for India had furnished him with material in the past, as in *The Sign of Four* and several short stories. Kipling, too, had turned to crime and detection in his early stories of Strickland of the Indian Police. The two writers got together and discussed the case, which was indeed a fascinating affair.

The scene was set in Mussoorie, a popular hill-station in the foothills of the Himalayas. It wasn't as grand as Simla (where the Viceroy and his entourage went) but it was a charming and convivial place, with a number of hotels and boarding-houses, a small military cantonment, and several private schools for European children.

It was during the summer 'season' of 1911 that Miss Frances Garnett-Orme came to stay in Mussoorie, taking a suite at the Savoy, a popular resort hotel. On 28 July she celebrated her 49th birthday. She was the daughter of George Garnett-Orme, of Skipton-in-Craven in Yorkshire, a district registrar of the Country Court. It was a family important enough to be counted among the landed gentry. Her father had died in 1892.

She came out to India in 1893 with the intention of marrying Jack Grant of the United Provinces Police. But he died in 1894 and she went back to England. Upset by his death following so soon after her father's, she turned to spiritualism in the hope of communicating with him. We must remember that spiritualism was all the rage in the early years of the century, seances and table-rappings being part of the social scene both in England and India. Madam Blavatsky, the chief exponent of spiritualism, was probably at the height of her popularity around this time; she spent her 'seasons' in neighbouring Simla, where she had many followers.

Miss Garnett-Orme's life was unsettled. She was drawn back to India, returning in 1901 to live in Lucknow, the regional capital of the United Provinces. She was still in contact with Jack Grant's family and saw his brother occasionally. The summer of 1907 was spent at Naini Tal, a hill-station popular with Lucknow residents. It was here that she met Miss Eva Mountstephen, who was working as a governess.

Eva Mountstephen, too, had an interest in spiritualism. It appears that she had actually told several of her friends about this time that she had learnt (in the course of a séancé) that in 1911 she would come into a great deal of money.

We are told that there was something sinister about Miss Mountstephen. She specialized in crystal-gazing, and what she saw in the glass often took a violent form. Her 'control', that is her connection in the spirit world, was a dead friend named Mrs Winter.

As a result of their common interest in the occult, Miss Garnett-Orme took on the younger woman as a companion when she returned to Lucknow in the winter. There they settled down together. But the summers were spent at one of the various hill-stations. Was there a latent lesbianism in their relationship? It was a restless, rootless life, but they were held together by the strong and heady influence of the séancé table and the crystal ball. Miss Garnett-Orme's indifferent health also made her dependent on the younger woman.

In the summer of 1911, the couple went up to Mussoorie, probably the most frivolous of hill-stations, where 'seasonal' love affairs were almost the order of the day. They took rooms in the Savoy. Electricity had yet to reach Mussoorie, and it was still the age of candelabras and gas-lit streets. Every house had a grand piano. If you didn't go out to a ball, you sang or danced at home. But Miss Garnett-Orme's spiritual pursuits took precedence over these more mundane entertainments. Towards the end of the 'season', on 12 September, Miss Mountstephen returned to Lucknow to pack up their household for a move to Jhansi, where they planned to spend the winter.

On the morning of 19 September, while Miss Mountstephen was still away, Miss Garnett-Orme was found dead in her bed. The door was locked from the inside. On her bedside table was a glass. She was positioned on the bed as though laid out by a nurse or undertaker.

Because of these puzzling circumstances, Major Birdwood of the Indian Medical Service (who was the Civil Surgeon in Mussoorie) was called in. He decided to hold an autopsy. It was discovered that Miss Garnett-Orme had been poisoned with prussic acid.

Prussic acid is a quick-acting poison, and would have killed too quickly for the victim to have composed herself in the way she was found. An ayah told the police that she had seen someone (she could not tell whether it was a man or a woman) slipping away through a large skylight and escaping over the roof.

Hill-stations are hotbeds of rumour and intrigue, and of course the gossips had a field day. Miss Garnett-Orme suffered from dyspepsia and was always dosing herself from a large bottle of Sodium Bicarbonate, which was regularly refilled. It was alleged that the bottle had been tampered with, that an unknown white powder had been added. Her doctor was questioned thoroughly. They even questioned a touring mind-reader, Mr Alfred Capper, who claimed that Miss Mountstephen had hurried from a room rather than have her mind read!

After several weeks the police arrested Miss Mountstephen. Although she had a convincing alibi (due to her absence in Jhansi) the police sought to prove that some kind of sinister influence had been exerted on Miss Garnett-Orme to take her medicine at a particular time. Thus, through suggestion, the murderer could kill and yet be away at the time of death. In her first novel, *The Mysterious Affair at Styles* (1920), the poisoner was in a distant place by the time her victim reached the fatal dose, the poison having precipitated to the bottom of the mixture. Perhaps Miss Christie read accounts of the Garnett-Orme case in the British press. Even the motive was similar.

But there was no Hercule Poirot in Mussoorie, and in court this theory could never be made convincing. The police case was never strong (they would have done better to have followed the ayah's lead), and it appears that they only acted because there was considerable ill-feeling in Mussoorie against Miss Mountstephen.

When the trial came up at Allahabad in March 1912, it caused a sensation. Murder by remote-control was something new in the annals of crime. But after hearing many days of evidence about the ladies' way of life, about crystal-gazing and premonitions of death, the court found Miss Mountstephen innocent. The Chief Justice, in delivering his verdict, remarked that the true circumstances of Miss Garnett-Orme's death would probably never be known. And he was right.

Miss Mountstephen applied for probate of her friend's will. But the Garnett-Orme family in England sent out her brother, Mr Hunter Garnett-Orme, to contest it. The case went in favour of Mr Garnett-Orme. The District Judge (W.D. Burkitt) turned down Miss Mountstephen's application on grounds of 'fraud and undue influence in connection with spiritualism and crystal gazing'. She went in appeal to the Allahabad High Court, but the Lower Court's decision was upheld.

Miss Mountstephen returned to England. We do not know her state of mind, but if she was innocent, she must have been a deeply embittered woman. Miss Garnett-Orme's doctor lost his flourishing practice in Mussoorie and left the country too. There were rumours that he and Miss Mountstephen had conspired to get hold of Miss Garnett-Orme's considerable fortune.

There was one more puzzling feature of the case. Mr Charles Jackson, a painter friend of many of those involved, had died suddenly, apparently of cholera, two months after Miss Garnett-Orme's mysterious death. The police took an interest in his sudden demise. When he was exhumed on 23 December, the body was found to be in a perfect state of preservation. He had died of arsenic poisoning.

Murder or suicide? This puzzle, too, was never resolved. Was there a connection with Miss Garnett-Orme's death? That too we shall never know. Had Conan Doyle taken up Kipling's suggestion and involved himself in the case (as he had done in so many others in England), perhaps the outcome would have been different.

As it is, we can only make our own conjectures.

The Death of Halpin Frayser

Ambrose Bierce

For by death is wrought greater change than hath been shown. Whereas in general the spirit that removed cometh back upon occasion, and is sometimes seen of those in flesh (appearing in the form of the body it bore) yet it hath happened that the veritable body without the spirit hath walked. And it is attested of those encountering who have lived to speak thereon that a lich so raised up hath no natural affection, nor remembrance thereof, but only hate. Also, it is known that some spirits which in life were benign become by death evil altogether.—*HALL*.

One dark night in midsummer a man waking from a dreamless sleep in a forest lifted his head from the earth, and staring a few moments into the blackness, said: 'Catharine Larue.' He said nothing more; no reason was known to him why he should have said so much.

The man was Halpin Frayser. He lived in St. Helena, but where he lives now is uncertain, for he is dead. One who practises sleeping in the woods with nothing under him but the dry leaves and the damp earth, and nothing over him but the branches from which the leaves have fallen and the sky from which the earth has fallen, cannot hope for great longevity, and Frayser had already attained the age of thirty-two. There are persons in this world, millions of persons, and far and away the best persons, who regard that as a very advanced age. They are the children. To those who view the voyage of life from the port of departure the bark that has accomplished any considerable distance appears already in close approach to the farther shore. However, it is not certain that Halpin Frayser came to his death by exposure.

He had been all day in the hills west of the Napa Valley, looking for doves and such small game as was in season. Late in the afternoon it had come on to be cloudy, and he had lost his bearings; and although he had only to go always downhill— everywhere the way to safety when one is lost—the absence of trails had so impeded him that he was overtaken by night while still in the forest. Unable in the darkness to penetrate the thickets of manzanita and other undergrowth, utterly bewildered and overcome with fatigue, he had lain down near the root of a large madrono and fallen into a dreamless sleep. It was hours later, in the very middle of the night, that one of God's mysterious messengers, gliding ahead of the incalculable host of his companions sweeping westward with the dawn line, pronounced the awakening word in the ear of the sleeper, who sat upright and spoke, he knew not why, a name, he knew not whose.

2

Halpin Frayser was not much of a philosopher, nor a scientist. The circumstance that, waking from a deep sleep at night in the midst of a forest, he had spoken aloud a name that he had not in memory and hardly had in mind did not arouse an enlightened curiosity to investigate the phenomenon. He thought it odd, and with a little perfunctory shiver, as if in deference to a seasonal presumption that the night was chill, he lay down again and went to sleep. But his sleep was no longer dreamless.

He thought he was walking along a dusty road that showed white in the gathering darkness of a summer night. Whence and whither it led, and why he travelled it, he did not know, though all seemed simple and natural, as is the way in dreams; for in the Land Beyond the Bed surprises cease from troubling and the judgment is at rest. Soon he came to a parting of the ways; leading from the highway was a road less travelled, having the appearance, indeed, of having been long abandoned, because, he thought, it led to something evil; yet he turned into it without hesitation, impelled by some imperious necessity.

As he pressed forward he became conscious that his way was haunted by invisible existences whom he could not definitely figure to his mind. From among the trees on either side he caught broken and incoherent whispers in a strange tongue which yet he partly understood. They seemed to him fragmentary utterances of a monstrous conspiracy against his body and soul.

It was now long after nightfall, yet the interminable forest through which he journeyed was lit with a wan glimmer having no point of diffusion, for in its mysterious lumination nothing cast a shadow. A shallow pool in the guttered depression of an old wheel rut, as from a recent rain, met his eye with a crimson gleam. He stooped and plunged his hand into it. It stained his fingers; it was blood! Blood, he then observed, was about him everywhere. The weeds growing rankly by the roadside showed it in blots and splashes on their big, broad leaves. Patches of dry dust between the wheel-ways were pitted and spattered as with a red rain. Defiling the trunks of the trees were broad maculations of crimson, and blood dripped like dew from their foliage.

3

All this he observed with a terror which seemed not incompatible with the fulfilment of a natural expectation. It seemed to him that it was all in expiation of some crime which, though conscious of his guilt, he could not rightly remember. To the menaces and mysteries of his surroundings the consciousness was an added horror. Vainly he sought, by tracing life backward in memory, to reproduce the moment of his sin; scenes and incidents came crowding tumultuously into his mind, one picture effacing another, or commingling with it in confusion and obscurity, but nowhere could he catch a glimpse of what he sought. The failure augmented his terror; he felt as one who has murdered in the dark, not knowing whom nor why. So frightful was the situation—the mysterious light burned with so silent and awful a menace; the noxious plants, the trees that by common consent are invested with a melancholy or baleful character, so openly in his sight conspired against his peace; from overhead and all about came so audible and startling whispers and the sighs of creatures so obviously not of earth—that he could endure it no longer, and with a great effort to break some malign spell that bound his faculties to silence and inaction, he shouted with the full strength of his lungs! His voice, broken, it seemed, into an infinite multitude of unfamiliar sounds, went babbling and stammering away into the distant reaches of the forest, died into silence, and all was as before. But he had made a beginning at resistance and was encouraged. He said:

'I will not submit unheard. There may be powers that are not malignant travelling this accursed road. I shall leave them a record and an appeal. I shall relate my wrongs, the persecutions that I endure—I, a helpless mortal, a penitent, an unoffending poet!'

Halpin Frayser was a poet only as he was a penitent: in his dream.

Taking from his clothing a small red-leather pocketbook one half of which was leaved for memoranda, he discovered that he was without a pencil. He broke a twig from a bush, dipped it into a pool of blood and wrote rapidly. He had hardly touched the paper with the point of his twig when a low, wild peal of laughter broke out at a measureless distance away, and growing ever louder, seemed approaching ever nearer; a soulless, heartless, and unjoyous laugh, like that of the loon, solitary by the lakeside at midnight; a laugh which culminated in an unearthly shout close at hand, then died away by slow gradations, as if the accursed being that uttered it had withdrawn over the verge of the world whence it had come. But the man felt that this was not so—that it was near by and had not moved.

4

A strange sensation began slowly to take possession of his body and his mind. He could not have said which, if any, of his senses was affected; he felt it rather as a consciousness—a mysterious mental assurance of some overpowering presence—some supernatural malevolence different in kind from the invisible existences that swarmed about him, and superior to them in power. He knew that it had uttered that hideous laugh. And now it seemed to be approaching him; from what direction he did not know—dared not conjecture. All his former fears were forgotten or merged in the gigantic terror that now held him in thrall. Apart from that, he had but one thought: to complete his written appeal to the benign powers who, traversing the haunted wood, might sometime rescue him if he should be denied the blessing of annihilation. He wrote with terrible rapidity, the twig in his fingers rilling blood without renewal; but in the middle of a sentence his hands denied their service to his will, his arms fell to his sides, the book to the earth; and powerless to move or cry out, he found himself staring into the sharply drawn face and blank, dead eyes of his own mother, standing white and silent in the garments of the grave!

II

In his youth Halpin Frayser had lived with his parents in Nashville, Tennessee. The Fraysers were well-to-do, having a good position in such society as had survived the wreck wrought by civil war. Their children had the social and educational opportunities of their time and place, and had responded to good associations and instruction with agreeable manners and cultivated minds. Halpin being the youngest and not over-robust was perhaps a trifle 'spoiled'. He had the double disadvantage of a mother's assiduity and a father's neglect. Frayser pere was what no Southern man of means is not—a politician. His country, or rather his section and State, made demands upon his time and attention so exacting that to those of his family he was compelled to turn an ear partly deafened by the thunder of the political captains and the shouting, his own included.

Young Halpin was of a dreamy, indolent and rather romantic turn, somewhat more addicted to literature than law, the profession to which he was bred. Among those of his relations who professed the modern faith of heredity it was well understood that in him the character of the late Myron Bayne, a maternal great-grandfather, had revisited the glimpses of the moon—by which orb Bayne had in his lifetime been sufficiently affected to be a poet of no small Colonial distinction. If not specially observed, it was observable that while a Frayser who was not the proud possessor of a sumptuous copy of the ancestral 'poetical works' (printed at the family expense, and long ago withdrawn from an inhospitable market) was a rare Frayser indeed, there was an illogical indisposition to honour the great deceased in the person of his spiritual successor. Halpin was pretty generally deprecated as an intellectual black sheep who was likely at any moment to disgrace the flock by bleating in metre. The Tennessee Fraysers were a practical folk—not practical in the popular sense of devotion to sordid pursuits, but having a robust contempt for any qualities unfitting a man for the wholesome vocation of politics.

5

In justice to young Halpin it should be said that while in him were pretty faithfully reproduced most of the mental and moral characteristics ascribed by history and family tradition to the famous Colonial bard, his succession to the gift and faculty divine was purely inferential. Not only had he never been known to court the Muse, but in truth he could not have written correctly a line of verse to save himself from the Killer of the Wise. Still, there was no knowing when the dormant faculty might wake and smite the lyre.

In the meantime the young man was rather a loose fish, anyhow. Between him and his mother was the most perfect sympathy, for secretly the lady was herself a devout disciple of the late and great Myron Bayne, though with the tact so generally and justly admired in her sex (despite the hardy calumniators who insist that it is essentially the same thing as cunning) she had always taken care to conceal her weakness from all eyes but those of him who shared it. Their common guilt in respect of that was an added tie between them. If in Halpin's youth his mother had 'spoiled' him he had assuredly done his part toward being spoiled. As he grew to such manhood as is attainable by a Southerner who does not care which way elections go, the attachment between him and his beautiful mother—whom from early childhood he had called Katy—became yearly stronger and more tender. In these two romantic natures was manifest in a signal way that neglected phenomenon, the dominance of the sexual element in all the relations of life, strengthening, softening, and beautifying even those of consanguinity. The two were nearly inseparable, and by strangers observing their manners were not infrequently mistaken for lovers.

Entering his mother's boudoir one day Halpin Frayser kissed her upon the forehead, toyed for a moment with a lock of her dark hair which had escaped from its confining pins, and said, with an obvious effort at calmness:

'Would you greatly mind, Katy, if I were called away to California for a few weeks?'

6

It was hardly needful for Katy to answer with her lips a question to which her tell-tale cheeks had made instant reply. Evidently she would greatly mind; and the tears, too, sprang into her large brown eyes as corroborative testimony.

'Ah, my son,' she said, looking up into his face with infinite tenderness, 'I should have known that this was coming. Did I not lie awake a half of the night weeping because, during the other half, Grandfather Bayne had come to me in a dream, and standing by his portrait—young, too, and handsome as that—pointed to yours on the same wall? And when I looked it seemed that I could not see the features; you had been painted with a face cloth, such as we put upon the dead. Your father has laughed at me, but you and I, dear, know that such things are not for nothing. And I saw below the edge of the cloth the marks of hands on your throat—forgive me, but we have not been used to keep such things from each other. Perhaps you have another interpretation. Perhaps it does not mean that you will go to California. Or maybe you will take me with you?'

It must be confessed that this ingenious interpretation of the dream in the light of newly-discovered evidence did not wholly commend itself to the son's more logical mind; he had, for the moment at least, a conviction that it foreshadowed a more simple and immediate, if less tragic, disaster than a visit to the Pacific Coast. It was Halpin Frayser's impression that he was to be garroted on his native heath.

'Are there not medicinal springs in California?' Mrs Frayser resumed before he had time to give her the true reading of the dream—'places where one recovers from rheumatism and neuralgia? Look—my fingers feel so stiff; and I am almost sure they have been giving me great pain while I slept.' She held out her hands for his inspection. What diagnosis of her case the young man may have thought it best to conceal with a smile the historian is unable to state, but for himself he feels bound to say that fingers looking less stiff, and showing fewer evidences of even insensible pain, have seldom been submitted for medical inspection by even the fairest patient desiring a prescription of unfamiliar scenes. The outcome of it was that of these two odd persons having equally odd notions of duty, the one went to California, as the interest of his client required, and the other remained at home in compliance with a wish that her husband was scarcely conscious of entertaining.

7

While in San Francisco Halpin Frayser was walking one dark night along the waterfront of the city, when, with a suddenness that surprised and disconcerted him, he became a sailor. He was in fact 'shanghaied' aboard a gallant ship, and sailed for a far country. Nor did his misfortunes end with the voyage; for the ship was cast ashore on an island of the South Pacific, and it was six years afterward when the survivors were taken off by a venturesome trading schooner and brought back to San Francisco.

Though poor in purse, Frayser was no less proud in spirit than he had been in the years that seemed ages and ages ago. He would accept no assistance from strangers, and it was while living with a fellow survivor near the town of St. Helena, awaiting news and remittances from home, that he had gone gunning and dreaming.

III

The apparition confronting the dreamer in the haunted wood—the thing so like, yet so unlike, his mother—was horrible! It stirred no love nor longings in his heart; it came unattended with pleasant memories of a golden past—inspired no sentiment of any kind; all the finer emotions were swallowed up in fear. He tried to turn and run from before it, but his legs were as lead; he was unable to lift his feet from the ground. His arms hung helpless at his sides; of his eyes only he retained control, and these he dared not remove from the lustreless orbs of the apparition, which he knew was not a soul without a body, but that most dreadful of all existences infesting that haunted wood—a body without a soul! In its blank stare was neither love, nor pity, nor intelligence—nothing to which to address an appeal for mercy. 'An appeal will not lie,' he thought, with an absurd reversion to professional slang, making the situation more horrible, as the fire of a cigar might light up a tomb.

For a time, which seemed so long that the world grew grey with age and sin, and the haunted forest, having fulfilled its purpose in this monstrous culmination of its terrors, vanished out of his consciousness with all its sights and sounds, the apparition stood within a pace, regarding him with the mindless malevolence of a wild brute; then thrust its hands forward and sprang upon him with appalling ferocity! The act released his physical energies without unfettering his will; his mind was still spellbound, but his powerful body and agile limbs, endowed with a blind, insensate life of their own, resisted stoutly and well. For an instant he seemed to see this unnatural contest between a dead intelligence and a breathing mechanism only as a spectator—such fancies are in dreams; then he regained his identity almost as if by a leap forward into his body, and the straining automaton had a directing will as alert and fierce as that of its hideous antagonist.

8

But what mortal can cope with a creature of his dream? The imagination creating the enemy is already vanquished; the combat's result is the combat's cause. Despite his struggles— despite his strength and activity, which seemed wasted in a void, he felt the cold fingers close upon his throat. Borne backward to the earth, he saw above him the dead and drawn face within a hand's-breadth of his own, and then all was black. A sound as of the beating of distant drums—a murmur of swarming voices, a sharp, far cry signing all to silence, and Halpin Frayser dreamed that he was dead.

IV

A warm, clear night had been followed by a morning of drenching fog. At about the middle of the afternoon of the preceding day a little whiff of light vapour—a mere thickening of the atmosphere, the ghost of a cloud—had been observed clinging to the western side of Mount St. Helena, away up along the barren altitudes near the summit. It was so thin, so diaphanous, so like a fancy made visible, that one would have said: 'Look quickly! in a moment it will be gone.'

In a moment it was visibly larger and denser. While with one edge it clung to the mountain, with the other it reached farther and farther out into the air above the lower slopes. At the same time it extended itself to north and south, joining small patches of mist that appeared to come out of the mountain-side on exactly the same level, with an intelligent design to be absorbed. And so it grew and grew until the summit was shut out of view from the valley, and over the valley itself was an ever-extending canopy, opaque and grey. At Calistoga, which lies near the head of the valley and the foot of the mountain, there were a starless night and a sunless morning. The fog, sinking into the valley, had reached southward, swallowing up ranch after ranch, until it had blotted out the town of St. Helena, nine miles away. The dust in the road was laid; trees were adrip with moisture; birds sat silent in their coverts; the morning light was wan and ghastly, with neither colour nor fire.

9

Two men left the town of St. Helena at the first glimmer of

dawn, and walked along the road northward up the valley toward Calistoga. They carried guns on their shoulders, yet no one having knowledge of such matters could have mistaken them for hunters of bird or beast. They were a deputy sheriff from Napa and a detective from San Francisco—Holker and Jaralson, respectively. Their business was man-hunting.

'How far is it?' inquired Holker, as they strode along, their feet stirring white the dust beneath the damp surface of the road.

'The White Church? Only a half mile farther,' the other answered. 'By the way,' he added, 'it is neither white nor a church; it is an abandoned schoolhouse, grey with age and neglect. Religious services were once held in it—when it was white, and there is a graveyard that would delight a poet. Can you guess why I sent for you, and told you to come armed?'

'Oh, I never have bothered you about things of that kind. I've always found you communicative when the time came. But if I may hazard a guess, you want me to help you arrest one of the corpses in the graveyard.'

'You remember Branscom?' said Jaralson, treating his companion's wit with the inattention that it deserved.

'The chap who cut his wife's throat? I thought; I wasted a week's work on him and had my expenses for my trouble. There is a reward of five hundred dollars, but none of us ever got a sight of him. You don't mean to say—'

'Yes, I do. He has been under the noses of you fellows all the time. He comes by night to the old graveyard at the White Church.'

'The devil! That's where they buried his wife.'

'Well, you fellows might have had sense enough to suspect

that he would return to her grave some time!'

10

'The very last place that anyone would have expected him to return to.'

'But you had exhausted all the other places. Learning your failure at them, I "laid for him" there.'

'And you found him?'

'Damn it! he found me. The rascal got the drop on me—regularly held me up and made me travel. It's God's mercy that he didn't go through me. Oh, he's a good one, and I fancy the half of that reward is enough for me if you're needy.'

Holker laughed good-humouredly, and explained that his creditors were never more importunate.

'I wanted merely to show you the ground, and arrange a plan with you,' the detective explained. 'I thought it as well for us to be armed, even in daylight.'

'The man must be insane,' said the deputy sheriff. 'The reward is for his capture and conviction. If he's mad he won't be convicted.'

Mr Holker was so profoundly affected by that possible failure of justice that he involuntarily stopped in the middle of the road, then resumed his walk with abated zeal.

'Well, he looks it,' assented Jaralson. 'I'm bound to admit that a more unshaven, unshorn, unkempt, and uneverything wretch I never saw outside the ancient and honourable order of tramps. But I've gone in for him, and can't make up my mind to let go. There's glory in it for us, anyhow. Not another soul knows that he is this side of the Mountains of the Moon.'

'All right,' Holker said; 'we will go and view the ground,' and he added, in the words of a once-favourite inscription for tombstones: '"where you must shortly lie"—I mean if old Branscom ever gets tired of you and your impertinent intrusion. By the way, I heard the other day that "Branscom" was not his real name.'

11

'What is?'

'I can't recall it. I had lost all interest in the wretch and it did not fix itself in my memory—something like Pardee. The woman whose throat he had the bad taste to cut was a widow when he met her. She had come to California to look up some relatives—there are persons who will do that sometimes. But you know all that.'

'Naturally.'

'But not knowing the right name, by what happy inspiration did you find the right grave? The man who told me what the name was said it had been cut on the headboard.'

'I don't know the right grave.' Jaralson was apparently a trifle reluctant to admit his ignorance of so important a point of his plan. 'I have been watching about the place generally. A part of our work this morning will be to identify that grave. Here is the White Church.'

For a long distance the road had been bordered by fields on both sides, but now on the left there was a forest of oaks, madronos, and gigantic spruces whose lower parts only could be seen, dim and ghostly in the fog. The undergrowth was, in places, thick, but nowhere impenetrable. For some moments

Holker saw nothing of the building, but as they turned into the woods it revealed itself in faint grey outline through the fog, looking huge and far away. A few steps more, and it was within an arm's length, distinct, dark with moisture, and insignificant in size. It had the usual country-schoolhouse form—belonged to the packing-box order of architecture; had an underpinning of stones, a moss-grown roof, and blank window spaces, whence both glass and sash had long departed. It was ruined, but not a ruin—a typical Californian substitute for what are known to guide-bookers abroad as 'monuments of the past'. With scarcely a glance at this uninteresting structure Jaralson moved on into the dripping undergrowth beyond.

'I will show you where he held me up,' he said. 'This is the graveyard.'

12

Here and there among the bushes were small enclosures containing graves, sometimes no more than one. They were recognized as graves by the discoloured stones or rotting boards at head and foot, leaning at all angles, some prostrate; by the ruined picket fences surrounding them; or, infrequently, by the mound itself showing its gravel through the fallen leaves. In many instances nothing marked the spot where lay the vestiges of some poor mortal—who, leaving 'a large circle of sorrowing friends,' had been left by them in turn—except a depression in the earth, more lasting than that in the spirits of the mourners. The paths, if any paths had been, were long obliterated; trees of a considerable size had been permitted to grow up from the graves and thrust aside with root or branch the enclosing fences.

Overall was that air of abandonment and decay which seems nowhere so fit and significant as in a village of the forgotten dead.

As the two men, Jaralson leading, pushed their way through the growth of young trees, that enterprising man suddenly stopped and brought up his shotgun to the height of his breast, uttered a low note of warning, and stood motionless, his eyes fixed upon something ahead. As well as he could, obstructed by brush, his companion, though seeing nothing, imitated the posture and so stood, prepared for what might ensue. A moment later Jaralson moved cautiously forward, the other following.

Under the branches of an enormous spruce lay the dead body of a man. Standing silent above it they noted such particulars as first strike the attention—the face, the attitude, the clothing; whatever most promptly and plainly answers the unspoken question of a sympathetic curiosity.

The body lay upon its back, the legs wide apart. One arm was thrust upward, the other outward; but the latter was bent acutely, and the hand was near the throat. Both hands were tightly clenched. The whole attitude was that of desperate but ineffectual resistance to—what?

Near by lay a shotgun and a game bag through the meshes of which was seen the plumage of shot birds. All about were evidences of a furious struggle; small sprouts of poison-oak were bent and denuded of leaf and bark; dead and rotting leaves had been pushed into heaps and ridges on both sides of the legs by the action of other feet than theirs; alongside the hips were unmistakable impressions of human knees.

13

The nature of the struggle was made clear by a glance at the dead man's throat and face. While breast and hands were white, those were purple—almost black. The shoulders lay upon a low mound, and the head was turned back at an angle otherwise impossible, the expanded eyes staring blankly backward in a direction opposite to that of the feet. From the froth filling the open mouth the tongue protruded, black and swollen. The throat showed horrible contusions; not mere finger-marks, but bruises and lacerations wrought by two strong hands that must have buried themselves in the yielding flesh, maintaining their terrible grasp until long after death. Breast, throat, face, were wet; the clothing was saturated; drops of water, condensed from the fog, studded the hair and moustache.

All this the two men observed without speaking—almost at a glance. Then Holker said:

'Poor devil! he had a rough deal.'

Jaralson was making a vigilant circumspection of the forest, his shotgun held in both hands and at full cock, his finger upon the trigger.

'The work of a maniac,' he said, without withdrawing his eyes from the enclosing wood. 'It was done by Branscom—Pardee.'

Something half hidden by the disturbed leaves on the earth caught Holker's attention. It was a red-leather pocketbook. He picked it up and opened it. It contained leaves of white paper for memoranda, and upon the first leaf was the name 'Halpin

Frayser.' Written in red on several succeeding leaves—scrawled as if in haste and barely legible—were the following lines, which Holker read aloud, while his companion continued scanning the dim grey confines of their narrow world and hearing matter of apprehension in the drip of water from every burdened branch:

'Enthralled by some mysterious spell, I stood
In the lit gloom of an enchanted wood.
The cypress there and myrtle twined their boughs,
Significant, in baleful brotherhood.

'The brooding willow whispered to the yew;
Beneath, the deadly nightshade and the rue,
With immortelles self-woven into strange
Funereal shapes, and horrid nettles grew.

'No song of bird nor any drone of bees,
Nor light leaf lifted by the wholesome breeze:
The air was stagnant all, and Silence was
A living thing that breathed among the trees.

'Conspiring spirits whispered in the gloom,
Half-heard, the stilly secrets of the tomb.
With blood the trees were all adrip; the leaves
Shone in the witch-light with a ruddy bloom.

'I cried aloud!—the spell, unbroken still,
Rested upon my spirit and my will.
Unsouled, unhearted, hopeless and forlorn,
I strove with monstrous presages of ill!
'At last the viewless—'

Holker ceased reading; there was no more to read. The manuscript broke off in the middle of a line.

'That sounds like Bayne,' said Jaralson, who was something of a scholar in his way. He had abated his vigilance and stood looking down at the body.

'Who's Bayne?' Holker asked rather incuriously.

'Myron Bayne, a chap who flourished in the early years of the nation—more than a century ago. Wrote mighty dismal stuff; I have his collected works. That poem is not among them, but it must have been omitted by mistake.'

'It is cold,' said Holker; 'let us leave here; we must have the coroner from Napa.'

14

Jaralson said nothing, but made a movement in compliance. Passing the end of the slight elevation of earth upon which the dead man's head and shoulders lay, his foot struck some hard substance under the rotting forest leaves, and he took the trouble to kick it into view. It was a fallen headboard, and painted on it were the hardly decipherable words, 'Catharine Larue.'

'Larue, Larue!' exclaimed Holker, with sudden animation. 'Why, that is the real name of Branscom—not Pardee. And— bless my soul! how it all comes to me—the murdered woman's name had been Frayser!'

'There is some rascally mystery here,' said Detective Jaralson. 'I hate anything of that kind.' There came to them out of the fog—seemingly from a great distance—the sound of a laugh, a low, deliberate, soulless laugh which had no more of joy than that of a hyena night-prowling in the desert; a laugh that rose by slow gradation, louder and louder, clearer, more distinct and terrible, until it seemed barely outside the narrow circle of their vision; a laugh so unnatural, so unhuman, so devilish, that it filled those hardy man-hunters with a sense of dread unspeakable! They did not move their weapons nor think of them; the menace of that horrible sound was not of the kind to be met with arms. As it had grown out of silence, so now it died away; from a culminating shout which had seemed almost in their ears, it drew itself away into the distance until its failing notes, joyous and mechanical to the last, sank to silence at a measureless remove.

The Lady or the Tiger

Frank Stockton

In the very olden time there lived a semi-barbaric king, whose ideas, though somewhat polished and sharpened by the progressiveness of distant Latin neighbours, were still large, florid, and untrammelled, as became the half of him which was barbaric. He was a man of exuberant fancy, and, withal, of an authority so irresistible that, at his will, he turned his varied fancies into facts. He was greatly given to self-communing, and, when he and himself agreed upon anything, the thing was done. When every member of his domestic and political systems moved smoothly in its appointed course, his nature was bland and genial; but, whenever there was a little hitch, and some of his orbs got out of their orbits, he was blander and more genial still, for nothing pleased him so much as to make the crooked straight and crush down uneven places.

Among the borrowed notions by which his barbarism had become semified was that of the public arena, in which, by exhibitions of manly and beastly valour, the minds of his subjects were refined and cultured.

But even here the exuberant and barbaric fancy asserted itself. The arena of the king was built, not to give the people an opportunity of hearing the rhapsodies of dying gladiators, nor to enable them to view the inevitable conclusion of a conflict between religious opinions and hungry jaws, but for purposes far better adapted to widen and develop the mental energies of the people. This vast amphitheatre, with its encircling galleries, its mysterious vaults, and its unseen passages, was an agent of poetic justice, in which crime was punished, or virtue rewarded, by the decrees of an impartial and incorruptible chance.

When a subject was accused of a crime of sufficient importance to interest the king, public notice was given that on an appointed day the fate of the accused person would be decided in the king's arena, a structure which well deserved its name, for, although its form and plan were borrowed from afar, its purpose emanated solely from the brain of this man, who, every barleycorn a king, knew no tradition to which he owed more allegiance than pleased his fancy, and who ingrafted on every adopted form of human thought and action the rich growth of his barbaric idealism.

When all the people had assembled in the galleries, and the king, surrounded by his court, sat high up on his throne of royal state on one side of the arena, he gave a signal, a door beneath him opened, and the accused subject stepped out into the amphitheatre. Directly opposite him, on the other side of the enclosed space, were two doors, exactly alike and side by side. It was the duty and the privilege of the person on trial to walk directly to these doors and open one of them.

He could open either door he pleased; he was subject to no guidance or influence but that of the aforementioned impartial and incorruptible chance. If he opened the one, there came out of it a hungry tiger, the fiercest and most cruel that could be procured, which immediately sprang upon him and tore him to pieces as a punishment for his guilt. The moment that the case of the criminal was thus decided, doleful iron bells were clanged, great wails went up from the hired mourners posted on the outer rim of the arena, and the vast audience, with bowed heads and downcast hearts, wended slowly their homeward way, mourning greatly that one so young and fair, or so old and respected, should have merited so dire a fate.

But, if the accused person opened the other door, there came forth from it a lady, the most suitable to his years and station that his majesty could select among his fair subjects, and to this lady he was immediately married, as a reward of his innocence. It mattered not that he might already possess a wife and family, or that his affections might be engaged upon an object of his own selection; the king allowed no such subordinate arrangements to interfere with his great scheme of retribution and reward. The exercises, as in the other instance, took place immediately, and in the arena. Another door opened beneath the king, and a priest, followed by a band of choristers, and dancing maidens blowing joyous airs on golden horns and treading an epithalamic measure, advanced to where the pair stood, side by side, and the wedding was promptly and cheerily solemnized. Then the gay brass bells rang forth their merry peals, the people shouted glad hurrahs, and the innocent man, preceded by children strewing flowers on his path, led his bride to his home.

This was the king's semi-barbaric method of administering justice. Its perfect fairness is obvious. The criminal could not know out of which door would come the lady; he opened either he pleased, without having the slightest idea whether, in the next instant, he was to be devoured or married. On some occasions the tiger came out of one door, and on some out of the other. The decisions of this tribunal were not only fair, they were positively determinate: the accused person was instantly punished if he found himself guilty, and, if innocent, he was rewarded on the spot, whether he liked it or not. There was no escape from the judgments of the king's arena.

The institution was a very popular one. When the people gathered together on one of the great trial days, they never knew whether they were to witness a bloody slaughter or a hilarious wedding. This element of uncertainty lent an interest to the occasion which it could not otherwise have attained. Thus, the masses were entertained and pleased, and the thinking part of the community could bring no charge of unfairness against this plan, for did not the accused person have the whole matter in his own hands?

This semi-barbaric king had a daughter as blooming as his most florid fancies, and with a soul as fervent and imperious as his own. As is usual in such cases, she was the apple of his eye, and was loved by him above all humanity. Among his courtiers was a young man of that fineness of blood and lowness of station common to the conventional heroes of romance who love royal maidens. This royal maiden was well satisfied with her lover, for he was handsome and brave to a degree unsurpassed in all this kingdom, and she loved him with an ardour that had enough of barbarism in it to make it exceedingly warm and strong. This love affair moved on happily for many months, until one day the king happened to discover its existence. He did not hesitate nor waver in regard to his duty in the premises. The youth was immediately cast into prison, and a day was appointed for his trial in the king's arena. This, of course, was an especially important occasion, and his majesty, as well as all the people, was greatly interested in the workings and development of this trial. Never before had such a case occurred; never before had a subject dared to love the daughter of the king. In after years such things became commonplace enough, but then they were in no slight degree novel and startling.

The tiger-cages of the kingdom were searched for the most savage and relentless beasts, from which the fiercest monster might be selected for the arena; and the ranks of maiden youth and beauty throughout the land were carefully surveyed by competent judges in order that the young man might have a fitting bride in case fate did not determine for him a different destiny. Of course, everybody knew that the deed with which the accused was charged had been done. He had loved the princess, and neither he, she, nor any one else, thought of denying the fact; but the king would not think of allowing any fact of this kind to interfere with the workings of the tribunal, in which he took such great delight and satisfaction. No matter how the affair turned out, the youth would be disposed off, and the king would take an aesthetic pleasure in watching the course of events, which would determine whether or not the young man had done wrong in allowing himself to love the princess.

The appointed day arrived. From far and near the people gathered, and thronged the great galleries of the arena, and crowds, unable to gain admittance, massed themselves against its outside walls. The king and his court were in their places, opposite the twin doors, those fateful portals, so terrible in their similarity.

All was ready. The signal was given. A door beneath the royal party opened, and the lover of the princess walked into the arena. Tall, beautiful, fair, his appearance was greeted with a low hum of admiration and anxiety. Half the audience had not known so grand a youth had lived among them. No wonder the princess loved him! What a terrible thing for him to be there!

As the youth advanced into the arena he turned, as the custom was, to bow to the king, but he did not think at all of that royal personage. His eyes were fixed upon the princess, who sat to the right of her father. Had it not been for the moiety of barbarism in her nature it is probable that lady would not have been there, but her intense and fervid soul would not allow her to be absent on an occasion in which she was so terribly interested. From the moment that the decree had gone forth that her lover should decide his fate in the king's arena, she had thought of nothing, night or day, but this great event and the various subjects connected with it. Possessed of more power, influence, and force of character than any one who had ever before been interested in such a case, she had done what no other person had done—she had possessed herself of the secret of the doors. She knew in which of the two rooms, that lay behind those doors, stood the cage of the tiger, with its open front, and in which waited the lady. Through these thick doors, heavily curtained with skins on the inside, it was impossible that any noise or suggestion should come from within to the person who should approach to raise the latch of one of them. But gold, and the power of a woman's will, had brought the secret to the princess.

And not only did she know in which room stood the lady ready to emerge, all blushing and radiant, should her door be opened, but she knew who the lady was. It was one of the fairest and loveliest of the damsels of the court who had been selected as the reward of the accused youth, should he be proved innocent of the crime of aspiring to one so far above him; and the princess hated her. Often had she seen, or imagined that she had seen, this fair creature throwing glances of admiration upon the person of her lover, and sometimes she thought these glances were perceived, and even returned. Now and then she had seen them talking together; it was but for a moment or two, but much can be said in a brief space; it may have been on most unimportant topics, but how could she know that? The girl was lovely, but she had dared to raise her eyes to the loved one of the princess; and, with all the intensity of the savage blood transmitted to her through long lines of wholly barbaric ancestors, she hated the woman who blushed and trembled behind that silent door.

When her lover turned and looked at her, and his eye met hers as she sat there, paler and whiter than any one in the vast ocean of anxious faces about her, he saw, by that power of quick perception which is given to those whose souls are one, that she knew behind which door crouched the tiger, and behind which stood the lady. He had expected her to know it. He understood her nature, and his soul was assured that she would never rest until she had made plain to herself this thing, hidden to all other lookers-on, even to the king. The only hope for the youth in which there was any element of certainty was based upon the success of the princess in discovering this mystery; and the moment he looked upon her, he saw she had succeeded, as in his soul he knew she would succeed.

Then it was that his quick and anxious glance asked the question: 'Which?' It was as plain to her as if he shouted it from where he stood. There was not an instant to be lost. The question was asked in a flash; it must be answered in another.

Her right arm lay on the cushioned parapet before her. She raised her hand, and made a slight, quick movement toward the right. No one but her lover saw her. Every eye but his was fixed on the man in the arena.

He turned, and with a firm and rapid step he walked across the empty space. Every heart stopped beating, every breath was held, every eye was fixed immovably upon that man. Without the slightest hesitation, he went to the door on the right, and opened it.

Now, the point of the story is this: Did the tiger come out of that door, or did the lady?

The more we reflect upon this question, the harder it is to answer. It involves a study of the human heart which leads us through devious mazes of passion, out of which it is difficult to find our way. Think of it, fair reader, not as if the decision of the question depended upon yourself, but upon that hot-blooded, semi-barbaric princess, her soul at a white heat beneath the combined fires of despair and jealousy. She had lost him, but who should have him?

How often, in her waking hours and in her dreams, had she started in wild horror, and covered her face with her hands as she thought of her lover opening the door on the other side of which waited the cruel fangs of the tiger!

But how much oftener had she seen him at the other door! How in her grievous reveries had she gnashed her teeth, and torn her hair, when she saw his start of rapturous delight as he opened the door of the lady! How her soul had burned in agony when she had seen him rush to meet that woman, with her flushing cheek and sparkling eye of triumph; when she had seen him lead her forth, his whole frame kindled with the joy of recovered life; when she had heard the glad shouts from the multitude, and the wild ringing of the happy bells; when she had seen the priest, with his joyous followers, advance to the couple, and make them man and wife before her very eyes; and when she had seen them walk away together upon their path of flowers, followed by the tremendous shouts of the hilarious multitude, in which her one despairing shriek was lost and drowned!

Would it not be better for him to die at once, and go to wait for her in the blessed regions of semi-barbaric futurity?

And yet, that awful tiger, those shrieks, that blood!

Her decision had been indicated in an instant, but it had been made after days and nights of anguished deliberation. She had known she would be asked, she had decided what she would answer, and, without the slightest hesitation, she had moved her hand to the right.

The question of her decision is one not to be lightly considered, and it is not for me to presume to set myself up as the one person able to answer it. And so I leave it with all of you: Which came out of the opened door—the lady, or the tiger?

The Man with the Pale Eyes

Guy de Maupassant

Monsieur Pierre Agénor De Vargnes, the Examining Magistrate, was the exact opposite of a practical joker. He was dignity, staidness, correctness personified. As a sedate man, he was quite incapable of being guilty, even in his dreams, of anything resembling a practical joke, however remotely. I know nobody to whom he could be compared, unless it be the present president of the French Republic. I think it is useless to carry the analogy any further, and having said thus much, it will be easily understood that a cold shiver passed through me when Monsieur Pierre Agénor de Vargnes did me the honour of sending a lady to await on me.

At about eight o'clock, one morning last winter, as he was leaving the house to go to the *Palais de Justice*, his footman handed him a card, on which was printed:

DOCTOR JAMES FERDINAND,
Member of the Academy of Medicine,
Port-au-Prince,
Chevalier of the Legion of Honour.

At the bottom of the card there was written in pencil:

From Lady Frogère.

Monsieur de Vargnes knew the lady very well, who was a very agreeable Creole from Hayti, and whom he had met in many drawing-rooms, and, on the other hand, though the doctor's name did not awaken any recollections in him, his quality and titles alone required that he should grant him an interview, however short it might be. Therefore, although he was in a hurry to get out, Monsieur de Vargnes told the footman to show in his early visitor, but to tell him beforehand that his master was much pressed for time, as he had to go to the Law Courts.

When the doctor came in, in spite of his usual imperturbability, he could not restrain a movement of surprise, for the doctor presented that strange anomaly of being a negro of the purest, blackest type, with the eyes of a white man, of a man from the North, pale, cold, clear, blue eyes, and his surprise increased, when, after a few words of excuse for his untimely visit, he added, with an enigmatical smile:

'My eyes surprise you, do they not? I was sure that they would, and, to tell you the truth, I came here in order that you might look at them well, and never forget them.'

His smile, and his words, even more than his smile, seemed to be those of a madman. He spoke very softly, with that childish, lisping voice, which is peculiar to negroes, and his mysterious, almost menacing words, consequently, sounded all the more as if they were uttered at random by a man bereft of his reason. But his looks, the looks of those pale, cold, clear, blue eyes, were certainly not those of a madman. They clearly expressed menace, yes, menace, as well as irony, and, above all, implacable ferocity, and their glance was like a flash of lightning, which one could never forget.

'I have seen,' Monsieur de Vargnes used to say, when speaking about it, 'the looks of many murderers, but in none of them have I ever observed such a depth of crime, and of impudent security in crime.'

And this impression was so strong, that Monsieur de Vargnes thought that he was the sport of some hallucination, especially as when he spoke about his eyes, the doctor continued with a smile, and in his most childish accents: 'Of course, Monsieur, you cannot understand what I am saying to you, and I must beg your pardon for it. Tomorrow you will receive a letter which will explain it all to you, but, first of all, it was necessary that I should let you have a good, a careful look at my eyes, my eyes, which are myself, my only and true self, as you will see.'

With these words, and with a polite bow, the doctor went out, leaving Monsieur de Vargnes extremely surprised, and a prey to this doubt, as he said to himself:

'Is he merely a madman? The fierce expression, and the criminal depths of his looks are perhaps caused merely by the extraordinary contrast between his fierce looks and his pale eyes.'

And absorbed in these thoughts, Monsieur de Vargnes unfortunately allowed several minutes to elapse, and then he thought to himself suddenly:

'No, I am not the sport of any hallucination, and this is no case of an optical phenomenon. This man is evidently some terrible criminal, and I have altogether failed in my duty in not arresting him myself at once, illegally, even at the risk of my life.'

The judge ran downstairs in pursuit of the doctor, but it was too late; he had disappeared. In the afternoon, he called on Madame Frogère, to ask her whether she could tell him anything about the matter. She, however, did not know the negro doctor in the least, and was even able to assure him that he was a fictitious personage, for, as she was well acquainted with the upper classes in Hayti, she knew that the Academy of Medicine at Port-au-Prince had no doctor of that name among its members. As Monsieur de Vargnes persisted, and gave descriptions of the doctor, especially mentioning his extraordinary eyes, Madame Frogère began to laugh, and said:

'You have certainly had to do with a hoaxer, my dear monsieur. The eyes which you have described are certainly those of a white man, and the individual must have been painted.'

On thinking it over, Monsieur de Vargnes remembered that the doctor had nothing of the negro about him, but his black skin, his woolly hair and beard, and his way of speaking, which was easily imitated, but nothing of the negro, not even the characteristic, undulating walk. Perhaps, after all, he was only a practical joker, and during the whole day, Monsieur de Vargnes took refuge in that view, which rather wounded his dignity as a man of consequence, but which appeased his scruples as a magistrate.

The next day, he received the promised letter, which was written, as well as addressed, in letters cut out of the newspapers. It was as follows:

'MONSIEUR : Doctor James Ferdinand does not exist, but the man whose eyes you saw does, and you will certainly recognize his eyes. This man has committed two crimes, for which he does not feel any remorse, but, as he is a psychologist, he is afraid of some day yielding to the irresistible temptation of confessing his crimes. You know better than anyone (and that is your most powerful aid), with what imperious force criminals, especially intellectual ones, feel this temptation. That great Poet, Edgar Poe, has written masterpieces on this subject, which express the truth exactly, but he has omitted to mention the last phenomenon, which I will tell you. Yes, I, a criminal, feel a terrible wish for somebody to know of my crimes, and when this requirement is satisfied, my secret has been revealed to a confidant, I shall be tranquil for the future, and be freed from this demon of perversity, which only tempts us once. Well! now that is accomplished. You shall have my secret; from the day that you recognize me by my eyes, you will try and find out what I am guilty of, and how I was guilty, and you will discover it, being a master of your profession, which, by the by, has procured you the honour of having been chosen by me to bear the weight of this secret, which now is shared by us, and by us two alone. I say, advisedly, *by us two alone.* You could not, as a matter of fact, prove the reality of this secret to anyone, unless I were to confess it, and I defy you to obtain my public confession, as I have confessed it to you, *and without danger to myself.'*

Three months later, Monsieur de Vargnes met Monsieur X—at an evening party, and at first sight, and without the slightest hesitation, he recognized in him those very pale, very cold, and very clear blue eyes, eyes which it was impossible to forget.

The man himself remained perfectly impassive, so that Monsieur de Vargnes was forced to say to himself:

'Probably I am the sport of an hallucination at this moment, or else there are two pairs of eyes that are perfectly similar in the world. And what eyes! Can it be possible?'

The magistrate instituted inquiries into his life, and he discovered this, which removed all his doubts.

Five years previously, Monsieur X—had been a very poor, but very brilliant medical student, who, although he never took his doctor's degree, had already made himself remarkable by his microbiological researches.

A young and very rich widow had fallen in love with him and married him. She had one child by her first marriage, and in the space of six months, first the child and then the mother died of typhoid fever, and thus Monsieur X—had inherited a large fortune, in due form, and without any possible dispute. Everybody said that he had attended to the two patients with the utmost devotion. Now, were these two deaths the two crimes mentioned in his letter?

But then, Monsieur X—must have poisoned his two victims with the microbes of typhoid fever, which he had skilfully cultivated in them, so as to make the disease incurable, even by the most devoted care and attention. Why not?

'Do you believe it?' I asked Monsieur de Vargnes.

'Absolutely,' he replied. 'And the most terrible thing about it is, that the villain is right when he defies me to force him to confess his crime publicly, for I see no means of obtaining a confession, none whatever. For a moment, I thought of magnetism, but who could magnetize that man with those pale, cold, bright eyes? With such eyes, he would force the magnetizer to denounce himself as the culprit.'

And then he said, with a deep sigh:

'Ah! Formerly there was something good about justice!'

And when he saw my inquiring looks, he added in a firm and perfectly convinced voice:

'Formerly, justice had torture at its command.'
'Upon my word,' I replied, with all an author's unconscious and simple egotism, 'it is quite certain that without the torture, this strange tale will have no conclusion, and that is very unfortunate, as far as regards the story I intended to make out of it.'

An Uncomfortable Bed

One autumn I went to stay for the hunting season with some friends in a chateau in Picardy.

My friends were fond of practical joking, as all my friends are. I do not care to know any other sort of people.

When I arrived, they gave me a princely reception, which at once aroused distrust in my breast. We had some capital shooting. They embraced me, they cajoled me, as if they expected to have great fun at my expense.

I said to myself:

'Look out, old ferret! They have something in preparation
for you.'

During the dinner, the mirth was excessive, far too great, in fact. I thought: 'Here are people who take a double share of amusement, and apparently without reason. They must be looking out in their own minds for some good bit of fun. Assuredly I am to be the victim of the joke. Attention!'

During the entire evening, everyone laughed in an exaggerated fashion. I smelled a practical joke in the air, as a dog smells game. But what was it? I was watchful, restless. I did not let a word or a meaning or a gesture escape me. Everyone seemed to me an object of suspicion, and I even looked distrustfully at the faces of the servants.

The hour rang for going to bed, and the whole household came to escort me to my room. Why? They called to me: 'Good night.' I entered the apartment, shut the door, and remained standing, without moving a single step, holding the wax candle in my hand.

I heard laughter and whispering in the corridor. Without doubt they were spying on me. I cast a glance around the walls, the furniture, the ceiling, the hangings, the floor. I saw nothing to justify suspicion. I heard persons moving about outside my door. I had no doubt they were looking through the keyhole.

An idea came into my head: 'My candle may suddenly go out, and leave me in darkness.'

Then I went across to the mantelpiece, and lighted all the wax candles that were on it. After that, I cast another glance around me without discovering anything. I advanced with short steps, carefully examining the apartment. Nothing. I inspected every article one after the other. Still nothing. I went over to the window. The shutters, large wooden shutters, were open. I shut them with great care, and then drew the curtains, enormous velvet curtains, and I placed a chair in front of them, so as to have nothing to fear from without.

Then I cautiously sat down. The armchair was solid. I did not venture to get into the bed. However, time was flying; and I ended by coming to the conclusion that I was ridiculous. If they were spying on me, as I supposed, they must, while waiting for the success of the joke they had been preparing for me, have been laughing enormously at my terror. So I made up my mind to go to bed. But the bed was particularly suspicious-looking. I pulled at the curtains. They seemed to be secure. All the same, there was danger. I was going perhaps to receive a cold shower-bath from overhead, or perhaps, the moment I stretched myself out, to find myself sinking under the floor with my mattress. I searched in my memory for all the practical jokes of which I ever had experience. And I did not want to be caught. Ah! certainly not! certainly not! Then I suddenly bethought myself of a precaution which I consider one of extreme efficacy: I caught hold of the side of the mattress gingerly, and very slowly drew it toward me. It came away, followed by the sheet and the rest of the bedclothes. I dragged all these objects into the very middle of the room, facing the entrance door. I made my bed over again as best I could at some distance from the suspected bedstead and the corner which had filled me with such anxiety. Then, I extinguished all the candles, and, groping my way, I slipped under the bedclothes.

For at least another hour, I remained awake, starting at the slightest sound. Everything seemed quiet in the chateau. I fell asleep.

I must have been in a deep sleep for a long time, but all of a sudden, I was awakened with a start by the fall of a heavy body tumbling right on top of my own body, and, at the same time, I received on my face, on my neck, and on my chest a burning liquid which made me utter a howl of pain. And a dreadful noise, as if a sideboard laden with plates and dishes had fallen down, penetrated my ears.

I felt myself suffocating under the weight that was crushing me and preventing me from moving. I stretched out my hand to find out what was the nature of this object. I felt a face, a nose, and whiskers. Then with all my strength I launched out a blow over this face. But I immediately received a hail of cuffings which made me jump straight out of the soaked sheets, and rush in my nightshirt into the corridor, the door of which I found open.

O stupor! it was broad daylight. The noise brought my friends hurrying into the apartment, and we found, sprawling over my improvised bed, the dismayed valet, who, while bringing me my morning cup of tea, had tripped over this obstacle in the middle of the floor, and fallen on his stomach, spilling, in spite of himself, my breakfast over my face.

The precautions I had taken in closing the shutters and going to sleep in the middle of the room had only brought about the interlude I had been striving to avoid.

Ah! how they all laughed that day!

The Mortal Immortal

Mary Shelley

July 16, 1833.—This is a memorable anniversary for me; on it
I complete my three hundred and twenty-third year!

The Wandering Jew?—certainly not. More than eighteen
centuries have passed over his head. In comparison with him,
I am a very young Immortal.

Am I, then, immortal? This is a question which I have asked
myself, by day and night, for now three hundred and three
years, and yet cannot answer it. I detected a grey hair amidst
my brown locks this very day—that surely signifies decay. Yet it
may have remained concealed there for three hundred years—
for some persons have become entirely white-headed before
twenty years of age.

I will tell my story, and my reader shall judge for me. I will
tell my story, and so contrive to pass some few hours of a long
eternity, become so wearisome to me. For ever! Can it be? to
live for ever! I have heard of enchantments, in which the victims
were plunged into a deep sleep, to wake, after a hundred years,
as fresh as ever: I have heard of the Seven Sleepers—thus to be

immortal would not be so burthensome: but, oh! the weight of never-ending time—the tedious passage of the still-succeeding hours! How happy was the fabled Nourjahad!——But to my task.

All the world has heard of Cornelius Agrippa. His memory is as immortal as his arts have made me. All the world has also heard of his scholar, who, unawares, raised the foul fiend during his master's absence, and was destroyed by him. The report, true or false, of this accident, was attended with many inconveniences to the renowned philosopher. All his scholars at once deserted him—his servants disappeared. He had no one near him to put coals on his ever-burning fires while he slept, or to attend to the changeful colours of his medicines while he studied. Experiment after experiment failed, because one pair of hands was insufficient to complete them: the dark spirits laughed at him for not being able to retain a single mortal in his service.

I was then very young—very poor—and very much in love. I had been for about a year the pupil of Cornelius, though I was absent when this accident took place. On my return, my friends implored me not to return to the alchemist's abode. I trembled as I listened to the dire tale they told; I required no second warning; and when Cornelius came and offered me a purse of gold if I would remain under his roof, I felt as if Satan himself tempted me. My teeth chattered—my hair stood on end:—I ran off as fast as my trembling knees would permit.

My failing steps were directed whither for two years they had every evening been attracted,—a gently bubbling spring of pure living waters, beside which lingered a dark-haired girl, whose beaming eyes were fixed on the path I was accustomed each night to tread. I cannot remember the hour when I did not love Bertha; we had been neighbours and playmates from infancy— her parents, like mine, were of humble life, yet respectable—our attachment had been a source of pleasure to them. In an evil hour, a malignant fever carried off both her father and mother, and Bertha became an orphan. She would have found a home beneath my paternal roof, but, unfortunately, the old lady of the near castle, rich, childless, and solitary, declared her intention to adopt her. Henceforth Bertha was clad in silk—inhabited a marble palace—and was looked on as being highly favoured by fortune. But in her new situation among her new associates, Bertha remained true to the friend of her humbler days; she often visited the cottage of my father, and when forbidden to go thither, she would stray towards the neighbouring wood, and meet me beside its shady fountain.

She often declared that she owed no duty to her new protectress equal in sanctity to that which bound us. Yet still I was too poor to marry, and she grew weary of being tormented on my account. She had a haughty but an impatient spirit, and grew angry at the obstacles that prevented our union. We met now after an absence, and she had been sorely beset while I was away; she complained bitterly, and almost reproached me for being poor. I replied hastily,—

'I am honest, if I am poor!—were I not, I might soon become rich!'

This exclamation produced a thousand questions. I feared to shock her by owning the truth, but she drew it from me; and then, casting a look of disdain on me, she said, 'You pretend to love, and you fear to face the Devil for my sake!'

I protested that I had only dreaded to offend her;—while she dwelt on the magnitude of the reward that I should receive. Thus encouraged—shamed by her—led on by love and hope, laughing at my late fears, with quick steps and a light heart, I returned to accept the offers of the alchemist, and was instantly installed in my office.

A year passed away. I became possessed of no insignificant sum of money. Custom had banished my fears. In spite of the most painful vigilance, I had never detected the trace of a cloven foot; nor was the studious silence of our abode ever disturbed by demoniac howls. I still continued my stolen interviews with Bertha, and Hope dawned on me—Hope—but not perfect joy; for Bertha fancied that love and security were enemies, and her pleasure was to divide them in my bosom. Though true of heart, she was somewhat of a coquette in manner; and I was jealous as a Turk. She slighted me in a thousand ways, yet would never acknowledge herself to be in the wrong. She would drive me mad with anger, and then force me to beg her pardon. Sometimes she fancied that I was not sufficiently submissive, and then she had some story of a rival, favoured by her protectress. She was surrounded by silk-clad youths—the rich and gay—What chance had the sad-robed scholar of Cornelius compared with these?

On one occasion, the philosopher made such large demands upon my time, that I was unable to meet her as I was wont. He was engaged in some mighty work, and I was forced to remain, day and night, feeding his furnaces and watching his chemical preparations. Bertha waited for me in vain at the fountain. Her haughty spirit fired at this neglect; and when at last I stole out during the few short minutes allotted to me for slumber, and hoped to be consoled by her, she received me with disdain, dismissed me in scorn, and vowed that any man should possess her hand rather than he who could not be in two places at once for her sake. She would be revenged!—And truly she was. In my dingy retreat I heard that she had been hunting, attended by Albert Hoffer. Albert Hoffer was favoured by her protectress, and the three passed in cavalcade before my smoky window. Methought that they mentioned my name—it was followed by a laugh of derision, as her dark eyes glanced contemptuously towards my abode.

Jealousy, with all its venom, and all its misery, entered my breast. Now I shed a torrent of tears, to think that I should never call her mine; and, anon, I imprecated a thousand curses on her inconstancy. Yet, still I must stir the fires of the alchemist, still attend on the changes of his unintelligible medicines.

Cornelius had watched for three days and nights, nor closed his eyes. The progress of his alembics was slower than he expected: in spite of his anxiety, sleep weighed upon his eyelids. Again and again he threw off drowsiness with more than human energy; again and again it stole away his senses. He eyed his crucibles wistfully. 'Not ready yet,' he murmured; 'will another night pass before the work is accomplished? Winzy, you are vigilant—you are faithful—you have slept, my boy—you slept last night. Look at that glass vessel. The liquid it contains is of a soft rose-colour: the moment it begins to change its hue, awaken me—till then I may close my eyes. First, it will turn white, and then emit golden flashes; but wait not till then;

when the rose-colour fades, rouse me.' I scarcely heard the last words, muttered, as they were, in sleep. Even then he did not quite yield to nature. 'Winzy, my boy,' he again said, 'do not touch the vessel—do not put it to your lips; it is a philter—a philter to cure love; you would not cease to love your Bertha—beware to drink!'

And he slept. His venerable head sunk on his breast, and I scarce heard his regular breathing. For a few minutes I watched the vessel—the rosy hue of the liquid remained unchanged. Then my thoughts wandered—they visited the fountain, and dwelt on a thousand charming scenes never to be renewed—never! Serpents and adders were in my heart as the word 'Never!' half formed itself on my lips. False girl!—false and cruel! Never more would she smile on me as that evening she smiled on Albert. Worthless, detested woman! I would not remain unrevenged—she should see Albert expire at her feet—she should die beneath my vengeance. She had smiled in disdain and triumph—she knew my wretchedness and her power. Yet what power had she?—the power of exciting my hate—my utter scorn—my—oh, all but indifference! Could I attain that—could I regard her with careless eyes, transferring my rejected love to one fairer and more true, that were indeed a victory!

A bright flash darted before my eyes. I had forgotten the medicine of the adept; I gazed on it with wonder: flashes of admirable beauty, more bright than those which the diamond emits when the sun's rays are on it, glanced from the surface of the liquid; an odour the most fragrant and grateful stole over my sense; the vessel seemed one globe of living radiance, lovely to the eye, and most inviting to the taste. The first thought, instinctively inspired by the grosser sense, was, I will—I must drink. I raised the vessel to my lips. 'It will cure me of love— of torture!' Already I had quaffed half of the most delicious liquor ever tasted by the palate of man, when the philosopher stirred. I started—I dropped the glass—the fluid flamed and glanced along the floor, while I felt Cornelius's gripe at my throat, as he shrieked aloud, 'Wretch! you have destroyed the labour of my life!'

The philosopher was totally unaware that I had drunk any portion of his drug. His idea was, and I gave a tacit assent to it, that I had raised the vessel from curiosity, and that, frighted at its brightness, and the flashes of intense light it gave forth, I had let it fall. I never undeceived him. The fire of the medicine was quenched—the fragrance died away—he grew calm, as a philosopher should under the heaviest trials, and dismissed me to rest.

I will not attempt to describe the sleep of glory and bliss which bathed my soul in paradise during the remaining hours of that memorable night. Words would be faint and shallow types of my enjoyment, or of the gladness that possessed my bosom when I woke. I trod air—my thoughts were in heaven. Earth appeared heaven, and my inheritance upon it was to be one trance of delight. 'This it is to be cured of love,' I thought; 'I will see Bertha this day, and she will find her lover cold and regardless: too happy to be disdainful, yet how utterly indifferent to her!'

The hours danced away. The philosopher, secure that he had once succeeded, and believing that he might again, began to concoct the same medicine once more. He was shut up with his books and drugs, and I had a holiday. I dressed myself with care; I looked in an old but polished shield, which served me for a mirror; methought my good looks had wonderfully improved. I hurried beyond the precincts of the town, joy in my soul, the beauty of heaven and earth around me. I turned my steps towards the castle—I could look on its lofty turrets with lightness of heart, for I was cured of love. My Bertha saw me afar off, as I came up the avenue. I know not what sudden impulse animated her bosom, but at the sight, she sprung with a light fawn-like bound down the marble steps, and was hastening towards me. But I had been perceived by another person. The old high-born hag, who called herself her protectress, and was her tyrant, had seen me, also; she hobbled, panting, up the terrace; a page, as ugly as herself, held up her train, and fanned her as she hurried along, and stopped my fair girl with a 'How, now, my bold mistress? whither so fast? Back to your cage—hawks are abroad!'

Bertha clasped her hands—her eyes were still bent on my approaching figure. I saw the contest. How I abhorred the old crone who checked the kind impulses of my Bertha's softening heart. Hitherto, respect for her rank had caused me to avoid the lady of the castle; now I disdained such trivial considerations. I was cured of love, and lifted above all human fears; I hastened forwards, and soon reached the terrace. How lovely Bertha looked! her eyes flashing fire, her cheeks glowing with impatience and anger, she was a thousand times more graceful and charming than ever—I no longer loved—Oh! no, I adored—worshipped—idolized her!

She had that morning been persecuted, with more than

usual vehemence, to consent to an immediate marriage with my rival. She was reproached with the encouragement that she had shown him—she was threatened with being turned out of doors with disgrace and shame. Her proud spirit rose in arms at the threat; but when she remembered the scorn that she had heaped upon me, and how, perhaps, she had thus lost one whom she now regarded as her only friend, she wept with remorse and rage. At that moment I appeared. 'O, Winzy!' she exclaimed, 'take me to your mother's cot; swiftly let me leave the detested luxuries and wretchedness of this noble dwelling—take me to poverty and happiness.'

I clasped her in my arms with transport. The old lady was speechless with fury, and broke forth into invective only when we were far on our road to my natal cottage. My mother received the fair fugitive, escaped from a gilt cage to nature and liberty, with tenderness and joy; my father, who loved her, welcomed her heartily; it was a day of rejoicing, which did not need the addition of the celestial potion of the alchemist to steep me in delight.

Soon after this eventful day, I became the husband of Bertha. I ceased to be the scholar of Cornelius, but I continued to be his friend. I always felt grateful to him for having, unawares, procured me that delicious draught of a divine elixir, which, instead of curing me of love (sad cure! solitary and joyless remedy for evils which seem blessings to the memory), had inspired me with courage and resolution, thus winning for me an inestimable treasure in my Bertha.

I often called to mind that period of trance-like inebriation with wonder. The drink of Cornelius had not fulfilled the task for which he affirmed that it had been prepared, but its effects were more potent and blissful than words can express.

They had faded by degrees, yet they lingered long—and painted life in hues of splendour. Bertha often wondered at my lightness of heart and unaccustomed gaiety; for, before, I had been rather serious, or even sad, in my disposition. She loved me the better for my cheerful temper, and our days were winged by joy.

Five years afterwards I was suddenly summoned to the bedside of the dying Cornelius. He had sent for me in haste, conjuring my instant presence. I found him stretched on his pallet, enfeebled even to death; all of life that yet remained animated his piercing eyes, and they were fixed on a glass vessel, full of a roseate liquid.

'Behold,' he said, in a broken and inward voice, 'the vanity of human wishes! a second time my hopes are about to be crowned, a second time they are destroyed. Look at that liquor—you remember five years ago I had prepared the same, with the same success;—then, as now, my thirsting lips expected to taste the immortal elixir—you dashed it from me! and at present it is too late.'

He spoke with difficulty, and fell back on his pillow. I could not help saying—

'How, revered master, can a cure for love restore you to life?'

A faint smile gleamed across his face as I listened earnestly to his scarcely intelligible answer. 'A cure for love and for all things—the Elixir of Immortality. Ah! if now I might drink, I should live for ever!'

As he spoke, a golden flash gleamed from the fluid; a well-remembered fragrance stole over the air; he raised himself, all weak as he was—strength seemed miraculously to re-enter his frame—he stretched forth his hand—a loud explosion startled me—a ray of fire shot up from the elixir, and the glass vessel which contained it was shivered to atoms! I turned my eyes towards the philosopher; he had fallen back—his eyes were glassy—his features rigid—he was dead!

But I lived, and was to live for ever! So said the unfortunate alchemist, and for a few days I believed his words. I remembered the glorious drunkenness that had followed my stolen draught. I reflected on the change I had felt in my frame—in my soul. The bounding elasticity of the one—the buoyant lightness of the other. I surveyed myself in a mirror, and could perceive no change in my features during the space of the five years which had elapsed. I remembered the radiant hues and grateful scent of that delicious beverage—worthy the gift it was capable of bestowing—I was, then, IMMORTAL!

A few days after I laughed at my credulity. The old proverb, that 'a prophet is least regarded in his own country,' was true with respect to me and my defunct master. I loved him as a man—I respected him as a sage—but I derided the notion that he could command the powers of darkness, and laughed at the superstitious fears with which he was regarded by the vulgar. He was a wise philosopher, but had no acquaintance with any spirits but those clad in flesh and blood. His science was simply human; and human science, I soon persuaded myself, could never conquer nature's laws so far as to imprison the soul for ever within its carnal habitation. Cornelius had brewed a soul-refreshing drink—more inebriating than wine—sweeter and more fragrant than any fruit: it possessed probably strong medicinal powers, imparting gladness to the heart and vigour to the limbs; but its effects would wear out; already were they diminished in my frame. I was a lucky fellow to have quaffed health and joyous spirits, and perhaps long life, at my master's hands; but my good fortune ended there: longevity was far different from immortality.

I continued to entertain this belief for many years. Sometimes a thought stole across me—was the alchemist indeed deceived? But my habitual credence was, that I should meet the fate of all the children of Adam at my appointed time—a little late, but still at a natural age. Yet it was certain that I retained a wonderfully youthful look. I was laughed at for my vanity in consulting the mirror so often, but I consulted it in vain—my brow was untrenched—my cheeks—my eyes—my whole person continued as untarnished as in my twentieth year.

I was troubled. I looked at the faded beauty of Bertha—I seemed more like her son. By degrees our neighbours began to make similar observations, and I found at last that I went by the name of the Scholar bewitched. Bertha herself grew uneasy. She became jealous and peevish, and at length she began to question me. We had no children; we were all in all to each other; and though, as she grew older, her vivacious spirit became a little allied to ill-temper, and her beauty sadly diminished, I cherished her in my heart as the mistress I had idolized, the wife I had sought and won with such perfect love.

At last our situation became intolerable: Bertha was fifty—I twenty years of age. I had, in very shame, in some measure adopted the habits of a more advanced age; I no longer mingled in the dance among the young and gay, but my heart bounded along with them while I restrained my feet; and a sorry figure I cut among the Nestors of our village. But before the time I mention, things were altered—we were universally shunned; we were—at least, I was—reported to have kept up an iniquitous acquaintance with some of my former master's supposed friends. Poor Bertha was pitied, but deserted. I was regarded with horror and detestation.

What was to be done? We sat by our winter fire—poverty had made itself felt, for none would buy the produce of my farm; and often I had been forced to journey twenty miles, to some place where I was not known, to dispose off our property. It is true we had saved something for an evil day—that day had come.

We sat by our lone fireside—the old-hearted youth and his antiquated wife. Again Bertha insisted on knowing the truth; she recapitulated all she had ever heard said about me, and added her own observations. She conjured me to cast off the spell; she described how much more comely grey hair were than my chestnut locks; she descanted on the reverence and respect due to age—how preferable to the slight regard paid to mere children: could I imagine that the despicable gifts of youth and good looks outweighed disgrace, hatred, and scorn? Nay, in the end I should be burnt as a dealer in the black art, while she, to whom I had not deigned to communicate any portion of my good fortune, might be stoned as my accomplice. At length she insinuated that I must share my secret with her, and bestow on her like benefits to those I myself enjoyed, or she would denounce me—and then she burst into tears.

Thus beset, me thought it was the best way to tell the truth. I revealed it as tenderly as I could, and spoke only of a very long life, not of immortality—which representation, indeed, coincided best with my own ideas. When I ended, I rose and said—

'And now, my Bertha, will you denounce the lover of your youth?—You will not, I know. But it is too hard, my poor wife, that you should suffer from my ill-luck and the accursed arts of Cornelius. I will leave you—you have wealth enough, and friends will return in my absence. I will go; young as I seem, and strong as I am, I can work and gain my bread among strangers, unsuspected and unknown. I loved you in youth; God is my witness that I would not desert you in age, but that your safety and happiness require it.'

I took my cap and moved towards the door; in a moment Bertha's arms were round my neck, and her lips were pressed to mine. 'No, my husband, my Winzy,' she said, 'you shall not go alone—take me with you; we will remove from this place, and, as you say, among strangers we shall be unsuspected and safe. I am not so very old as quite to shame you, my Winzy; and I dare say the charm will soon wear off, and, with the blessing of God, you will become more elderly-looking, as is fitting; you shall not leave me.'

I returned the good soul's embrace heartily. 'I will not, my Bertha; but for your sake I had not thought of such a thing. I will be your true, faithful husband while you are spared to me, and do my duty by you to the last.'

The next day we prepared secretly for our emigration. We were obliged to make great pecuniary sacrifices—it could not be helped. We realized a sum sufficient, at least, to maintain us while Bertha lived; and, without saying adieu to any one, quitted our native country to take refuge in a remote part of western France.

It was a cruel thing to transport poor Bertha from her native village, and the friends of her youth, to a new country, new language, new customs. The strange secret of my destiny rendered this removal immaterial to me; but I compassionated her deeply, and was glad to perceive that she found compensation for her misfortunes in a variety of little ridiculous circumstances. Away from all tell-tale chroniclers, she sought to decrease the apparent disparity of our ages by a thousand feminine arts— rouge, youthful dress, and assumed juvenility of manner. I could not be angry—Did not I myself wear a mask? Why quarrel with hers, because it was less successful? I grieved deeply when I remembered that this was my Bertha, whom I had loved so fondly, and won with such transport—the dark eyed, dark- haired girl, with smiles of enchanting archness and a step like a fawn—this mincing, simpering, jealous old woman. I should have revered her grey locks and withered cheeks; but thus!—It was my work, I knew; but I did not the less deplore this type of human weakness.

Her jealousy never slept. Her chief occupation was to discover that, in spite of outward appearances, I was myself growing old. I verily believe that the poor soul loved me truly in her heart, but never had woman so tormenting a mode of displaying fondness. She would discern wrinkles in my face and decrepitude in my walk, while I bounded along in youthful vigour, the youngest looking of twenty youths. I never dared address another woman: on one occasion, fancying that the belle of the village regarded me with favouring eyes, she bought me a grey wig. Her constant discourse among her acquaintances was, that though I looked so young, there was ruin at work within my frame; and she affirmed that the worst symptom about me was my apparent health. My youth was a disease, she said, and I ought at all times to prepare, if not for a sudden and awful death, at least to awake some morning white-headed, and bowed down with all the marks of advanced years. I let her talk—I often joined in her conjectures. Her warnings chimed in with my never-ceasing speculations concerning my state, and I took an earnest, though painful, interest in listening to all that her quick wit and excited imagination could say on the subject.

Why dwell on these minute circumstances? We lived on for many long years. Bertha became bedridden and paralytic: I nursed her as mother might a child. She grew peevish, and still harped upon one string—of how long I should survive her. It has ever been a source of consolation to me, that I performed my duty scrupulously towards her. She had been mine in youth, she was mine in age, and at last, when I heaped the sod over her corpse, I wept to feel that I had lost all that really bound me to humanity.

Since then how many have been my cares and woes, how few and empty my enjoyments! I pause here in my history—I will pursue it no further. A sailor without rudder or compass, tossed on a stormy sea—a traveller lost on a widespread heath, without landmark or star to him—such have I been: more lost, more hopeless than either. A nearing ship, a gleam from some far cot, may save them; but I have no beacon except the hope of death.

Death! mysterious, ill-visaged friend of weak humanity! Why alone of all mortals have you cast me from your sheltering fold? O, for the peace of the grave! the deep silence of the iron-bound tomb! that thought would cease to work in my brain, and my heart beat no more with emotions varied only by new forms of sadness!

Am I immortal? I return to my first question. In the first place, is it not more probable that the beverage of the alchemist was fraught rather with longevity than eternal life? Such is my hope. And then be it remembered that I only drank half of the potion prepared by him. Was not the whole necessary to complete the charm? To have drained half the Elixir of Immortality is but to be half immortal—my For-ever is thus truncated and null.

But again, who shall number the years of the half of eternity? I often try to imagine by what rule the infinite may be divided. Sometimes I fancy age advancing upon me. One grey hair I have found. Fool! Do I lament? Yes, the fear of age and death often creeps coldly into my heart; and the more I live, the more I dread death, even while I abhor life. Such an enigma is man—born to perish—when he wars, as I do, against the established laws of his nature.

But for this anomaly of feeling surely I might die: the medicine of the alchemist would not be proof against fire—sword—and the strangling waters. I have gazed upon the blue depths of many a placid lake, and the tumultuous rushing of many a mighty river, and have said, peace inhabits those waters; yet I have turned my steps away, to live yet another day. I have asked myself, whether suicide would be a crime in one to whom thus only the portals of the other world could be opened. I have done all, except presenting myself as a soldier or duellist, an object of destruction to my—no, not my fellow-mortals, and therefore I have shrunk away. They are not my fellows. The inextinguishable power of life in my frame, and their ephemeral existence, place us wide as the poles asunder. I could not raise a hand against the meanest or the most powerful among them.

Thus I have lived on for many a year—alone, and weary of myself—desirous of death, yet never dying—a mortal immortal. Neither ambition nor avarice can enter my mind, and the ardent love that gnaws at my heart, never to be returned—never to find an equal on which to expend itself—lives there only to torment me.

This very day I conceived a design by which I may end all— without self-slaughter, without making another man a Cain—an expedition, which mortal frame can never survive, even endued with the youth and strength that inhabits mine. Thus I shall put my immortality to the test, and rest for ever—or return, the wonder and benefactor of the human species.

Before I go, a miserable vanity has caused me to pen these pages. I would not die, and leave no name behind. Three centuries have passed since I quaffed the fatal beverage: another year shall not elapse before, encountering gigantic dangers— warring with the powers of frost in their home—beset by famine, toil, and tempest—I yield this body, too tenacious a cage for a soul which thirsts for freedom, to the destructive elements of air and water—or, if I survive, my name shall be recorded as one of the most famous among the sons of men;

and, my task achieved, I shall adopt more resolute means, and, by scattering and annihilating the atoms that compose my frame, set at liberty the life imprisoned within, and so cruelly prevented from soaring from this dim earth to a sphere more congenial to its immortal essence.